RIDING THE NIGHT MARE

Edited by

Claire Savage

GW00701599

First published in Great Britain in 2001 by
POETRY NOW
Remus House,
Coltsfoot Drive,
Peterborough, PE2 9JX
Telephone (01733) 898101
Fax (01733) 313524

HB ISBN 0 75432 640 3
SB ISBN 0 75432 643 8

FOREWORD

'Brevity is the soul of wit'

A poet can say in thirty lines what it takes a novelist to say in 200 pages, is a comment that has been bandied about for centuries. The ability to express an emotion or describe a momentous event in a few lines has shown a facility for language, a vocabulary to be envied and an ear for the music of words. All qualities associated with the finest poets.

What about writers of prose? Surely those of us that find pleasure in prose still possess all of the skills mentioned above? With this in mind we decided to put our prose writers to the test and created a new challenge using the 'snapper', a 250 word short story.

The spine chiller seemed to be the perfect place to start. What a test of skills this would be. Could our writers send a shiver down our spines in 250 words or less? As you will read, they rose to the challenge and have proved that once the imagination has been engaged and a picture formed in the mind, the skilled writer of prose can create a fully rounded world in few words.

CONTENTS

SPINE-CHILLER

The pines had been purposely planted in their particular position in order to provide protection from prying eyes. For the stranger sheltering in the shack they signalled safety.

The power of the sun was not able to penetrate the canopy, but the glow of the golden orb gave guidance to Christel and Neil as they ambled aimlessly, lost in each other's lingering looks.

Hansel and Gretel-like in their innocence; Romeo and Juliet-like in their love, they were being drawn into a disturbing and dangerous density.

A whispering wall wended its way towards them

> O when will my love's journey end?
> O find me a road without bend!
> I need to avenge and amend.

Neil reluctantly released his hold on Christel's hand. His entreaties and endeavours were empty. Wondering why he was weeping, helpless to hold on to her, he watched as she merged with the mist which mingled with the ivy entwining itself around her fragile figure.

Fearful phrases fractured his feeble frame of mind.

> Where, O where is my beautiful bride?
> Why, O why does she wander and hide?
> She must with me, forever abide!

Neil edged ever onward.

Upon entering the shack, he was catapulted into a cave, where he was confronted by an avenging adversary, who was standing statuesque-like over his silent sweetheart. Desmond had stabbed her in the stomach with a stalactite.

Powerless to protect his princess he impaled himself on a stalagmite and joined her in eternity.

Desmond was doomed.

Catherine Craft

SLEEPING PARTNERS

Paul woke suddenly to his wife, not pushing *him,* but some nameless intruder in her dreams. Becky's sleep was restless again, perhaps due to the stress of moving house. She hadn't been herself lately.

She was calm now. Paul sat up and looked at her. 'She's beautiful,' he thought, 'I hope she feels better soon.'

A breeze brought goose-bumps out on Paul's arms. He thought he had shut the window - perhaps it was loose in the frame. He shivered and pulled the covers closer round Becky, but to his surprise, she was warm. Beads of sweat dotted her neck and face. She was murmuring something unintelligible. His brow creased in concern. Maybe she was coming down with flu.

Paul got out of bed and went to fetch her a glass of cold water. He shivered again as he went back into the bedroom.

Becky was lying just as he had left her, except her hair . . . her hair . . . Paul froze. Someone, *something,* was stroking his wife's long hair. He watched as the strap of her nightdress rolled down, watched the bedclothes mould to her figure.

Shapes, *legs,* shifted under the covers on Paul's side of the bed, the depression in his pillow moved, deepened. Becky's face tilted upwards - as if a hand cupped her chin. She was poised, *prepared . . .*

'*No!*' she protested, in barely a whisper, eyes still closed.

The glass fell, shattered into a myriad glittering, spiteful pieces, and made no difference to the night.

Sue Oldham

MAN-EATER

'Oh, new boy here's spotted Janice,' chortled Frank.
'Don't think about it, Joe. She's got a reputation.'

Ah, but some people won't be told, and Janice was a woman who would linger in the thoughts of many a man. Lithe, slim, with the strut of a predatory animal, perfume a slight musk. Joe though, had the soul of a big-game hunter.

So spoor was tracked, pit dug, bait pegged out. At the right moment Joe asked Janice out. She weighed him up. Slowly said yes.

Before the meal Joe admired the sheath of silk that was her calf-length dress. Later, he drove her home, kissed her lightly on the lips, cheek, behind the ear, but was pushed away when he moved towards the nape of her neck.
'Come in,' she whispered.

Coffee in hand, Joe sat on a broad leather sofa. Janice stood in the doorway.
'Weren't you warned about me?'
'Oh yes,' he murmured.
The dress slid down her body. Naked, she stepped forward, raised her hands to the hair behind her head and pulled the wood from the leather barrette. As her hair fell forward, so did her skin. Like a snake, the thin flesh fell in a single piece from a frame that was now revealed to be much leaner, much sharper.
'Didn't they tell you I was a man-eater?'
Wide-eyed, he stammered his reply. 'They said, they said it, but,' and pulling the layers from his own head, 'I didn't dare hope we'd be so well suited.'

Cardinal Cox

BLIND DATE

She came alone. Waiters guided her to the darkened alcove I had selected, out of sight of other diners, though I saw them, despite the gloom. Sara was pretty by mortal standards. I quoted my letter to prove that I was indeed J Asgaroth Cthulu, her date from the Love-Craft Dating Agency. She held my hand. Just in time I retracted my extra fingers. She took writhing flesh for nervousness and assured me that I had nothing to fear from her. I moved my chair back so she could not touch my face. I spoke, trying not to hiss or lisp.

'You list Madness among your hobbies on your character profile. That is why we are deemed so compatible.' She blathered on about Suggs and a House Of Fun. I discovered with horror that her 'Madness' were musicians. I almost induced her briefly with a gift of sight, to be removed the instant she saw me, leaving that the only true visual image in her head. Instead I left quietly, having settled the bill. I was stared at by a priest near the exit, who peered through the shrouds I cloaked myself in. Seeing he ate squid, I resurrected it (both what was on his plate and already swallowed) and left to the sound of his screams as fellow diners rushed too late to his aid.

I stepped into the night, and beyond. I will ask the Love-Craft people to arrange another blind date soon.

Arthur Chappell

THE SÉANCE

Roland Bernhart scrutinised each person at the dimly lit table.

And he saw the same thing in every face. Hope. They'd all come to him for the same reason, so distraught by the death of their loved ones they'd do anything. And Bernhart was happy to oblige . . . for a price.

In the relatively short space of time he'd been in this line of work, he'd made so much more than he ever had as the Great Alonzo's protégé-cum-lackey.

'You're tampering with forces you cannot possibly comprehend,' Alonzo had told him when he discovered his plans. But Bernhart understood the psychic game better than anyone realised. It was simply another con, another magic trick. The illusion of life after death.

He almost grinned as he instructed his clients to hold hands. Then Bernhart depressed the first button under his chair with his foot and it suddenly went icy cold - thanks to a small hidden fan in the room.

Bernhart rolled his eyes and groaned. 'Is there anybody out there? Knock once for yes, twice for no.'

His foot hovered over the second button, the one that triggered the tape player and the knocking sound effects. But before he could do anything, there came a sharp rap on the table. The sound went right through him and he jumped.

The tape player must've started on its own . . .

But no. Deep down Bernhart knew the truth.

There *was* somebody, some*thing* out there tonight . . .

And now it was in here.

With him.

P Kane

WHAT GOES AROUND COMES AROUND

The beast ripped at her neck unleashing a bubbling froth of dark blood. Her eyes stared with the clarity of the dying, yet her warm lips still found the power to scream one last protest.

A sound like thunder on the edge of perception and the scream yielded to darkness.

John allowed himself a small grin. He usually loved these old 'B' movie shock-horrors, but it was late and tiredness beat behind his eyes. He let out a leonine yawn and stretched against his inner opponent.

Rising, he crossed the small but cosy living room. Automatically his finger rested on the light switch as it had innumerable times. Tonight against all prior complacency, John hesitated. He felt a peculiar disquietude as if in the neonatal silence stalked an abyssal assassin. Shrugging defensively, John resisted the absurdity of the notion. Still the light remained infusing the room with warmth, like solace.

John's timorous mood led him dawdling across the room; alert and tense like a deer seeking a hunter. Then it hit him; or rather he hit it. He walked straight into an obstacle that wasn't there. His hands worked fretfully across the smooth invisible wall. Like a spouting geyser, panic burst through. Frantically his mind raced to find an explanation that didn't sound like something from one of his sci-fi shows.

He wailed in distress. Grease and sweat from his hands seemed to cling preternaturally to the air.

John heard a sound like thunder.

The screen went dead.

Peter Walton

HE THOUGHT HE WAS . . . BUT HE WASN'T

He stared at the corner of the room. Something had caught his attention; perhaps a slight movement or a rustling; or was it his imagination? Then, as he fought to pierce the gloom, the darkness seemed to solidify and to take shape. Suddenly, it sprang at him and attached itself to his face. Screaming with fear, he clawed at the thing as he felt a bite.

Then, incanting a half-forgotten prayer, he wrenched the thing from his face and hurled it into the fire. He heard a soggy splat and a sizzle, accompanied by the stench of putrid, burning flesh.

Mad with terror and convinced that his very soul was threatened, he ran from the room, flinging aside furniture and gabbling incoherently. Once in the cool evening air, his spirits rose and he felt a smidgen of hope.

Then it dawned on him that there were no lights anywhere - not in the street nor at any window. There was no traffic. There was no life. He did not exist.

Bill Paterson

ONE LAST COFFEE

The train lurched and Mr Edwards, sipping his coffee, swore as the hot liquid spilt over his trousers. 'Blast!' he exclaimed. The three strangers sitting at his table were suddenly united in sympathy.

'Bad luck!' said one. 'Here!' said another and handed him a serviette.

'For a moment' said Mr Edwards, mopping himself up, 'I thought we were going to be another statistic!' His companions laughed. The tall man in the seat by the window cleared his throat. 'And me with this year's sales forecast still to do!' he exclaimed.

Another laugh went round the table.

Mr Edwards finished his clean-up. He reached for his cup again.

'Are we slowing down?' he asked.

The man opposite lowered his paper. 'It'll be for the next stop!' he grunted.

Mr Edwards frowned. 'We aren't *supposed* to stop until Newcastle!' he complained. 'More engineering work, I bet - another delay! As if we haven't had enough!'

He had the cup nearly to his lips when the train jerked again as it stopped, sending another cascade of coffee on to his already damp trousers. He leapt to his feet. 'Oh, for God's sake!' he shouted.

And a deep booming voice rang out 'Did somebody mention my name?'

The men looked at each other. For suddenly, there was nothing else to look at . . .

Far away, in another world, they were removing the first of four bodies from the wreckage of the restaurant car . . .

R P Brown

PAN-IC

The girl entered the night-wrapped wood as though afraid to wake some sleeping demon, her footfalls silent and her breath quick and shallow.

Driven on by some unknown compulsion, she pushed her way through the brambles which seemed to reach out to trap and imprison her, the thorns scratching her hands and face, leaving tiny trickles of red rivulets as proof of their intent.

Deep into the trees she tip-toed, her heart pounding, her pulse racing at each movement within the leaves and bushes, as voles and night birds, at ease with the darkness, acted out their night games.

Shadows wound round her, eerily reminiscent of wraiths and goblins to her fevered imagination, and a soft wind rustled through the trees, mimicking ghostly echoes of her name.

The moon, pale and unhelpful, peeped out from the dark clouds overhead, and she saw in front of her a clearing, in the centre of which stood a blasted oak, its poisoned roots stretching many feet around the shattered trunk. She lurched forward, grateful for the break from thorns and shadows . . . and then, looking up, she saw him.

The great god Pan, he of the cloven hoof and pagan horns, leaning against the blackened body of the oak, his eyes bright in their intensity.

He raised his arms to her in welcome. 'So,' he said softly, 'you have come at last!'

And as he folded her into his embrace, her scream filled the world . . .

Anne Rolfe-Brooker

TERROR ON CLEE

A silver moon that night on Clee. A sleepy village lying at the door of death. No one knows or even suspects that the long deserted quarry is awake, but not for miners' work tonight. No picks or shovels, no ponies, no gaudy local chatter, but a shroud of funereal black descends the stairway of the lonely promontory surrounded not by sea, but meadowland, farms and cottages.

The air is cold and a circle of people draped in dull, dismal garb stand wild-eyed, firelight illuminates their faces for a second against the starlit sky, while strange chanting, unearthly moans and devilish shrieks transcend the night.

Maureen couldn't sleep, her mind full of deep foreboding. Something had woken her, a sense, a feeling, no, more than that, it was a presence. The house seemed solemn and empty, every noise, creaking floorboard, cooling pipe, set her nerves on edge. She got out of bed. The strange noise continued, somewhere outside towards the garden shed, a sort of rustling sound. Maybe she should wake her husband Bill? He was so tired, no, she would check herself. She carefully unlocked the back door . . .

Bill came to with a start. What was that sound? A scream? He looked over to his wife. She wasn't there. The house felt cold. He went downstairs.
'Maureen!' he called. 'Maureen, are you there, love?' No reply. The silence troubled him. He went to the kitchen and found the back door wide open. Morning air chilled him. He went outside and shouted again. Silence.

Nigel Latham

THE SHADOW

In the dark it is acceptable to have silly fancies - but not in daylight. Jane had loved the house when she first saw it, like a child's drawing, with central door and windows each side. Inside it had been less welcoming. It had been empty over a year and was bound to feel a bit cold and damp. She wanted to move. So why the reluctance? Why the unease?

While Dan and the children were there it was all right, but on Sunday he took them to the match, leaving her to get on. Then the empty house took her prisoner, trapped her in her own fears. She stayed safely in the kitchen, washing dishes, cleaning the surfaces, until after about an hour she realised that she needed a pee. She waited, hoping for Dan and the children to return, but eventually she had to go.

Jan took the stairs two at a time, and reached the sanctuary of the bathroom. She bolted the door. On the landing a tall, dark shadow hovered.

For half an hour Jane sat in the bathroom, shaking. On the landing the shadow waited patiently, a shadow not cast by any light.

At last the front door slammed, voices shouted, 'Mum, Mum, where are you?' And soundlessly the shadow vanished.

Jane was free, to go down and smile and pretend. Tomorrow she would wave them off to school. Tomorrow she would be alone in the house, haunted by silly fancies that did not fear the daylight.

Ann Harrison

A TWENTIES DRAMA

It was morning when he was taken from the house and escorted to a new rendezvous. Gas lamps still flickered in many of the houses along the way as he was urged, stumbling, to meet a prearranged deadline.

They stopped at a large building which, from its elevated position, seemed to crouch, sphinx-like, dominating all it surveyed. Built of smooth sandstone and glazed brick it looked smugly self-satisfied and at the same time vaguely threatening, like a sleek cat at a mousehole.

The main entrance was through a tall stone archway and after opening its squeaking iron gate, the escort led him across an expanse of concrete. Their steps echoed off the hard surface and he had an uneasy feeling that unseen eyes were watching his every step. The door carried a heavy black knocker made from cast iron and fashioned to represent a loop of rope. It hung from the door like a hangman's noose dangling from a gibbet. The escort banged it urgently three times.

An authorititive voice commanded them to enter and they stepped into a small office-like room, lit by a single gas mantle. The owner of the voice was a stout middle-aged lady, dressed entirely in black, with a loop of pearls around her neck which reached down to her waist. She and the escort whispered together for a moment and then, to his horror, the small boy realised that his mother was handing him over to a Headmistress. It was his first day at school.

Frank Jensen

LUCY

The horrors of the world outside can't penetrate the four walls of a cul-de-sac house.

Furious drivers who shout and swear, children who hurl abuse at pensioners and the ever present spectre of crime are locked outside. It was the fears Lucy was shut inside with which prompted her terror-edged breathing and rising panic.

Alone and locked in, she attempted to occupy her mind with a month-old magazine but nothing could hold her fear-laced attention. Her eyes just darted from one corner of the room to another.

Photographs came to life. Long dead relatives moved from their fixed poses, addicting Lucy to their cold eyes. The warm summer air gave way to a sinister cold that gently touched her fingers before creeping along her arm and spreading to blanket her lonely form. As the street noises began to vanish, they were replaced with the amplified sounds that echo through homes late at night. The boiler, the dripping tap, the picture falling from the mantelpiece. The picture falling? Lucy's panic began to rise now. Her eyes darted around the room more rapidly, her vision shooting from wall to wall, from photograph to photograph. But she couldn't leave yet.

The next ten minutes lasted an eternity. The clock struck eleven. In an uncertain stillness, time stopped. The atmosphere became colder and colder. Slowly, very slowly, Lucy rose and made her way to her husband's photograph over the fireplace.

The house was empty again.

Paul Benton

IT COULD BE YOU OR ME

As I fought my way through the undergrowth, I felt fear for the first time within my body.

For I knew I had but one chance to survive. It will be me or the wolf that would come out of the forest that night.

All I have is two rocks to help me.

Then I heard a rustle in the undergrowth. Is that the wolf or another frightened animal like me?

It was cold out and yet I could feel the sweat running down my face and a cold feeling down my back, one I had not felt in so many years.

Then all of a sudden, there before me stood a large black wolf, eyes shining bright and teeth that seemed to shine in the moonlight.

He started to show his teeth and snarling as if he knew the fear that was within my soul. All was so quiet, so quiet that I could hear the beating of my heart.

I asked myself, why must it be this way, why must we live in fear that a stranger may strike at any time of day or night?

We stood there it seemed for eternity, looking at each other. I turned and walked away thinking if he will attack, I would not see him coming. I did not hear a sound, only my heart beating, then I realised the only wolf in the forest was within myself.

Paul Volante

I'LL BE WAITING FOR YOU

Fred had forgotten what the constant nagging had been like. For three years he had enjoyed the quietness.
He ignored the loathing in her eyes, it didn't matter as long as she kept her mouth closed.

He had just settled down to read his paper when she spoke. It was the first words she had uttered since that terrible night.
'Don't think I've forgiven you, Fred Davies.' Her voice was brittle.
Fred dropped his paper. He stared at his wife in horror.
'Now then Molly, it was an accident.'
'Accident my eye. You knew what you were doing, you just weren't man enough to own up.'
Fred put his hands over his ears.
'Go away,' he moaned. 'Please go away.'
He was almost sobbing.
Molly stood up, brushing down her skirt with one skeletal hand.
'No Fred, I'm not going anywhere without you. I'll always be here, there is no escape.'

Silently she left the room.

Fred began to shake. Molly had been right, it hadn't been an accident; forty years of verbal abuse had finally tipped him over the edge.
He had removed the light on the landing and stairs and crouching in the dark he had waited for his wife. Just a little push was all it had taken.

As he reached the top of the stairs, an ice-cold draught touched his face.
In terror, he took a step backwards into oblivion.
The last voice he heard was his wife's.
'I'll be waiting for you Fred.'

Jacky Stevens

BRASSICA BLUES

The moon cast a pale blue light over the landscape as he set off for his usual walk. Everything seemed different to him tonight. The curved grasses shone silver-blue, and the trees were indigo against the darkening sky.

He came to a field of cabbages and began to walk along the edge. How strange they seemed, heads with no bodies, just thin, scrawny necks. He looked closer, surely that one had a face? He could see the curve of an ear, a lifted eyebrow, a mouth puckered into a sneer. He walked on quickly, feeling uneasy. That small one over there had sunken eyes and a chin-up, defiant appearance. How queer they looked, all nodding together. One very large one eyed him malevolently, an evil glare in its pale eyes. Another, further on, had a jester's frill round its neck, and a huge, gaping grin. He walked faster. He felt slightly nervous though he knew, of course, there was nothing to fear.

Then a small breeze sprang up, and at once he could hear them whispering, their heads turned together in pairs, gossiping maliciously - talking about *him*. An old head, heavily veined about the cheeks, leaned towards him and with curled lips showed undisguised contempt. He turned to go, and the whispering increased. Suddenly he was aware of movement, they were all facing towards him, slowly advancing across the field in the blue moonlight. Almost imperceptibly they crept on, shuffling gently and converging on the spot where he stood.

With a cry he fled, along the road, back up the lane, almost falling in his haste to be away from them. He could still hear the rustling sound as they marched quietly and steadily in his direction.

He reached the kitchen door and crashed inside, breathing heavily, wild hair across his eyes. His wife looked up from the table where she was preparing supper.

'You look as though you've seen a ghost!' she laughed. 'Never mind, we're having your favourite - sausage, mash and cabbage.' As she brought the knife blade down rapidly, chopping, he whirled round, pressing his hands over his ears.

He couldn't bear the sound of the screams.

Nancy Johnson

COMING HOME

A chill of fear came over me as I walked down the narrow footpath that wound its way past the ruins that had once been a lovely old church. Daylight was fading fast and the air around me felt cold and damp. In the overgrown churchyard, broken headstones stood like disfigured dwarfs from a fairytale, the hallowed ground no longer sacred, desecrated by the evils of the occult. Where hymns and psalms had once echoed, the sound of chanting and wailing now filled the air.

Lifeless eyes peered at me through the gloom. An owl hooted mournfully as the terrors of the night closed around me.

My heart began to beat like a drum, a cold sweat flooded my body at the sound of muffled footsteps somewhere close by.

I ran, stumbling over the rough ground. The footsteps sounded louder, accompanied by the laboured breathing of a dying soul struggling for life.

I turned round. A large black shape stood before me, a faceless being barring my way. The footsteps drew closer. I felt the hot rasping breath on my neck as an unseen hand touched my shoulder.

Paralysed with fear, I would move neither forwards nor backwards as the bony fingers encircled my throat.

I thought of my family waiting at home. For a brief moment I saw my children running towards me. I stretched out my hand but could not touch them.

Darkness engulfed me like a shroud.

Mummy would not be coming home tonight.

Jenny Porteous

I Never Thought It Would Be Like This!

It was her favourite place in all the world - Venice - and strangely the pain had gone. She smiled as eager trippers jostled to get their first sights of the mosaics in the Basilica, Tintoretto's 'Paradise' and, of course, the Bridge of Sighs. She stood in dazzling sunlight beyond the Rialto Bridge gazing at the Ca D'Or across the Grand Canal. But it was time to leave the crowds and discover again 'her' Venice.

It was suddenly colder, darker. Shivering, she drew her stole closer around her frail body. Leaving the raucous Bartolomeo Square she slipped into the world of narrow twisting walkways and tiny church-dominated campos, joining the handful of Venetians scurrying home as darkness fell. An hour passed - she was now far away from sights and sounds. The chatter and the footsteps of the locals had stopped. A rat slid with a 'plop' into the canal near her feet. She was alone and afraid.

She stumbled on - down this calle, along that salizzada. How could 'her' Venice be this cruel to her, she thought? But then suddenly she found herself on the familiar Misericordia Bridge and beyond it, bathed in glorious moonlight, was the great sweep of the lagoon.

All her fear drained away. Her body was weightless. The gondolier held out a hand and she stepped nimbly into the white gondola. As she floated out to the Cemetery of the Island of San Michele she whispered contentedly 'I never thought it would be like this!'

Peter Davies

STUCK IN THE MIDDLE

She sat in the corner motionless, knees hugged tightly to her chest. Silent. Her vacant eyes stared at the grimy floor which, although it was concrete, wasn't cold. However, being as numb as she was, she couldn't feel the floor, having succumbed to pins and needles some hours ago, nor the unexpected heat, nor the pain that she was storing behind the brick wall that she had erected to block out reality.

The screams in the distance, the lone shot that rang out in the immediate vicinity, the distinctive crackling; it all served to heighten her trance.

Others broke down with terror, pleading and praying for a saviour, or an end to this nightmare. Still she sat, she was consumed by her own world, ignoring the plight of the woman who was trying to protect the children from the flames that licked their arms.

The elderly man was down on his arthritic knees, pleading with the gunman to spare him, to remove the authoritative pistol from his temple. The manic cackle proved begging had been in vain, the power-crazed gunman playing God.

Finally, she looked up as the room fell silent, as figures ceased to move and animation became extinct. Her trance was broken.
'God, you are such a wuss Alicia. It's a game, nothing serious,' the boy standing over her cackled. Several others seemed to splutter in unison, but she couldn't see them.
'It's not fair! You know we don't like this . . . '

The final shot rang out.

Louise Crowley

UNTITLED

He reached the downtown hotel after midnight, and had to wake the sleepy hall-porter to be shown to his room, on the top floor. Switching on the bedside light, he was not encouraged by its feeble ray, which served only to cast uncertain shadows. In a dark corner, he noticed a large, old-fashioned cupboard, where he decided to hang his coat. He moved towards it, but as he touched the handle of the door, a soft, invisible hand closed firmly over his own. He was quite alone in the room, which had suddenly become chilly. The hand was unseen, but its presence was undeniable.

He pulled open the cupboard door. On a shelf inside the cupboard, a previous guest had left a battered, broken suitcase. Firmly, the invisible hand impelled him towards it, and forced his shaking fingers to fumble at the catches. He lifted the lid. As he did so, he heard a sob from some incorporeal presence beside him.

As the lid was raised, a tiny, dead hand, the hand of a dead baby, fell limply towards him . . .

Audrey J Smith

DO YOU BELIEVE IN GHOSTS?

I was challenged to spend the night at a reputedly haunted manor house, unoccupied by humans for some years.

I asked my girl Jill Jenkins to join me. I also invited the challengers to put up a fiver each, for charity. There were ground rules. No torches, candles, etc.

I arranged to meet Jill there. We each had a back door key. It was growing dark and I was first. I settled in the dining room. Later I heard Jill at the back door I'd left unlocked.

She seemed nervous and distant, but gripped my arm fiercely. The place was alive with noises. Skitterings in the chimney. Scuttlings in the wainscoting. Then the clank of chains! That wasn't explainable. Neither was the sudden chill in the air. Were we still alone?

Jill crept closer. She shivered and so did I. We clung desperately. Then she drew away.

I relaxed and must have fallen asleep. I awoke with sunlight coming through the grimy panes. I'd survived, but I was alone and the back door was locked. No need for that - or to have gone off without a word. I'd have something to say, later.

I went home and after a drink I fell into bed and was awoken by the phone. It was Jill.
'Sorry I couldn't come last night. I had a lousy cold and temperature and couldn't face it!'
I mumbled something and replaced the phone, thoughtfully.
If Jill didn't come, who had I been clinging to all night?

James Kimber

ONE SUMMER NIGHT

While holidaying late summer, a year or two ago, in a cottage, it being basic. Not far from a village on the coast it was. On the seafront, one evening when dusk was setting in the sea, mist was coming in, like a thick fog.

I had to go to the village for something, it was about a twenty minute walk into the village. The mist was getting thicker, a chill in the air, it being late evening, I could hear the sea.

I started to visualise some dark shape ahead of me, like a village, but it was ten minutes away, still voice panic shouting. I started to sweat, cold shivers down my spine.

What was happening? The village, my cottage. Where . . . where was it? Was it my imagination? I began to breathe heavily. What was happening? Cold, I felt the mist, voices, the sea, was I lost? Those voices of panic shouting in the distance.

What was this all about? Clammy I was now. Get a grip, I said to myself. Carrying on walking, the mist still thick. The village had been flooded some time in the past, a century or so back in time when it was a stormy night. I somehow walked into a village churchyard, gravestones, mist looking at one . . . No! It can't be, help!

That had been one hell of a bad dream. No more lager and curry before bedtime.

Arthur May

THE GATE

Walking through the forest, I had now reached the large imperious gate that led to 'the house'. I hesitated for a moment. Should I go inside? I leant against the high, decaying wall that was covered with creeping vines and stared at the gate.

Afraid, but inquisitive, I knew I just had to open this gate and see what was in there. Now almost dark with just a half moon looking down sardonically, watching my trembling frame.

Inhaling deeply, I suddenly lunged forward and with a mighty shove turned the latch and pushed open the gate, creeping inside. An owl hooted. The trees rustled menacingly. The gate screeched.

Unable to close my mouth, I stood there with my eyes screwed up, shivers running along my spine. Finally I opened my eyes and glared through the darkness at my surroundings. The long, unkempt path seemed to beckon me, showing me the way to the great house. The haunted house. Should I go on? Far easier to turn round and run back out again.

Great hulking trees casting eerie shadows in the moonlight either side of the path, were bending and pointing their gnarled fingers at me. The hairs on the back of my neck were stretched with fear.

I was sure the house was moving nearer, getting bigger. It wanted to devour me. I screamed out in terror, my stomach twisting in knots.

Quickly I turned back and yanked at the latch on the gate again. But it remained solid and unyielding. Locked. I was shut in.
Trapped.

Linda Hurdwell

CATASTROPHE

It was the first time Meredith Drew had worked alone after the museum closed. The Egyptian section in which she was situated reeked of ancient corpses. Various statues of deity and sarcophagi filled every available space. The glass showcases were illuminated, highlighting the displays where the past reverberated with the present. It was to be a delicate task unravelling the bandages of the mummy set before her upon the table. It would need a steady hand and dedication. In a way it was quite macabre and she could not help but think of the curse of pharaoh Tutankhamen.

As she painstakingly plied the bandages away, she felt as though someone was watching her every move and a chill ran up her spine. At intervals within the wrapping, amulets were placed as protection for the soul of the departed. As she removed the final bandage and canvas shroud, revealed were the features of an unknown young woman.

She walked across the room to get the four canopic jars which held the deceased's organs. Suddenly a loud crash made Meredith stop in her tracks, heart pounding in her chest as she called out 'Who's there?' receiving no answer.

She saw that one of the terracotta jars lay broken on the floor, its contents strewn around. She felt the colour drain from her cheeks as something brushed past her ankle. 'A curse,' she murmured, fainting.

Tut-Ankh, the museum cat, stepped across her still body and playfully reached out his paw. *Miaow.*

Ann G Wallace

NOCTAMBULATION

The stagecoach was late leaving the Red Lion Inn. A horse had lost a shoe and the farrier had been delayed. Darkness falls early in winter. Every trace of daylight had gone when Emily stepped down and waved goodbye to the coachman.

She was going to visit friends at Woodside farm. It was in a lonely and isolated place. It could be reached either by a long walk up Cathole Lane and through Dye Works yard, or by a shorter walk through the wood. The wood had been familiar to her since childhood and she strode off in that direction.

She passed the big house on her left, the dam on her right and followed the hawthorn hedge to the stile. Minutes later she heard a twig snap and footsteps approaching. A shape loomed out of the gloom. She was on the point of shouting 'Walter' when she realised that this silhouette belonged to a stranger.

Praying earnestly that she hadn't been seen, she hid in undergrowth. She mustn't sneeze or cough or even breathe audibly. The tall man made his way to the stile and then proceeded. Thankful for her soft soles, Emily ran to the edge of the wood, over the bridge and across the field. There were no candles lit in the front windows. She raised her hand to knock and then heard footsteps behind her. Hardly daring to look, she saw a shaft of lantern light and heard a welcoming bark. 'Walter, Tess, thank goodness.'

Vivienne Brocklehurst

THE DRAGON MAN

'Mummy! Mummeeee!'

'Leave him Clare,' Dave growled.

'Mummy! Mummeeee!' Clare raced upstairs.

It was cold. The curtains billowed. 'Mummy!' Simon reached out.

'Mummy's here,' she murmured. 'What is it?'

'The dragon man was here!'

Clare tucked him up again. 'It was only a dream,' she soothed. The window rattled and shook. She shut it.

'The dragon man opened it, Mummy,' Simon whispered.

'Go to sleep,' Clare crooned. The boy relaxed and closed his eyes.

All was calm now. The curtains hung limp and the room felt warmer. *Crash!* Clare gasped as the mobile fell.

'Mummy! Is that the dragon man again?' Simon breathed.

'No, of course not,' she soothed. 'Your mobile fell - that's all.'

He shivered. Cold seeped around them. She hugged Simon to her. The curtains flapped furiously. The door opened. Simon screamed.

'Stop this nonsense Simon!' Dave thundered. 'Let go of your mother and lie down!' Clare clutched him to her.

'Mummy! Mummeee! It's him. It's the dragon man!' Clare pulled the boy to face her.

'You know it's only Daddy.'

A deep chuckle made her turn. Distorted laughter echoed around the room. Sparks flashed and flames shot from his mouth.

Simon went rigid, his ashen face contorted with fear as the dragon man grabbed him. Clare screamed.

'You've always babied him,' Dave sneered. 'I'll teach him how to fly with the devil!'

A blinding flash, then he smashed through the rattling window, green-scaled wings beating as he flew off with his son into the night.

Kath Hurley

LOST IN TIME

I'd been driving for what seemed like hours, black menacing clouds had gathered, spots of rain appeared on my windscreen quickly turning to heavy torrential rain. I decided to stop and waited for the rain to subside.

After a while the rain eased off and I was able to see clearly. I continued on my journey but soon realised I was completely lost. In the distance was a light shining and as I got closer I saw a storm lantern in an upstairs window of a large, rambling old house. 'Must be there for lost travellers' I mused. 'I'll call and ask for directions.' After ringing the doorbell and waiting for some time, the door opened slowly to reveal a tall shadowy figure in long, dark clothes. I was about to speak but recoiled in horror when I saw the figure had no face, only a hole where a nose should be. I wanted to run, I could feel the thing's foul smelling breath on me. It was pulling at my clothes. I tried to scream, felt as if I was suffocating. I must have fainted, the next thing I knew I found myself back in the car. A torch was being shone in my face. 'Are you alright Miss?' a voice said.

'Yes thank you Officer,' I answered weakly. 'Just a bad dream.' Or was it?

Gloria Wilkes

SOMEWHERE; BEYOND THE SEA

Day 21:
They're all dead now. Starvation; or so they thought. At least I won't
starve; not when I've got my ship mates.

Day 22:
I've just finished off Smithy. Very nice; very tasty. He was so
succulent, like the best roast pork you ever tasted. There's only Tyler
and McCraig left; but they should last me until we reach land. I hope
Tyler isn't too sinewy. I'm looking forward to McCraig though, lots of
meat on him; I'll save him till last.

Day 25:
Just McCraig left now; I'll start him tomorrow.

Day 25:
'Somewhere; beyond the sea. She's there waiting for me. La la de de
de.'
Who's singing? Did McCraig just move?

Day 25:
What the hell!

Day 26:
'Somewhere; beyond the sea. She's there waiting for me. My lover
stands on golden sands; and watches the ships that go sailin'.'

Rachel C Zaino

DON'T BE AFRAID OF THE DARK

She loved the night. Just as well. She was at one with the night. But she shouldn't be out, the papers were full of killings. A local man they thought. Someone who knew his victims, perhaps a student.

Then curfews. Chaste young women should stay in. She had wanted to see the film though. It had been better than the usual ones.

She had to walk home along dark North Road, past the old hospital grounds. She was enjoying the feeling of the night, of the stars.

'Hello sexy,' He steps out of the shadow. She looks quickly up and down the street. No one.
'We're all alone,' he says.
She recognises the voice. The lecturer in English. This man teaches the students he's killed. She goes to evening classes of his.

Still no one in the road but them.
'You shouldn't have broken curfew. There's always one who doesn't listen.'

Hands on her neck.

'Neither should you have broken curfew.'

His eyes widen. He sees starlight reflected on the two gleaming teeth, just before they sink into his neck.

She loves the night. There is always so much food about.

Melanie M Burgess

His Last Chance

Brrr!

It was winter. A raw sea coldness rolled in carrying a wave-top mist above a fast incoming tide. On the shore he was fishing with a handline. He stood on the outer sandbank where mounting waves kept sweeping his line sideways. He hauled and rebaited.

Splash!

A good cast over the choppy sea, further than he could throw a cricket ball. As the wind-flung waves cavorted he was determined to stay to win his supper. He swung his arms across his chest to keep warm.

The line swayed and dragged under the tide's energy. A sudden jerk on his numbing fingers registered a bite. He pulled in his line slowly, failing to notice the increasing width and depth of the rapidly filling pool between him and the main beach.

A large wave came annoyingly filling his boots.

Two limp hooks appeared but the third was trailing something which didn't flap but swirled dark brown in the swishing water. He spent some time disentangling a very large crab lassoed by one big claw. He bagged his 'catch'.

His feet ached with cold. His absorption had befuddled his reason.

Packing up, he then tried to cross the deepening pool. Suddenly he began sinking into wet sand up to his thighs. He roared a shout. Struggling, he sank up to his waist. Moments later icy water flowed across his chest.

The crab floated away as if waving its claws. Foam filled his ears as his neck chilled. His brain clouded.

Dennis Marshall

A Vision In Black

Staring at the wall with a glazed look it was obvious that her mind was elsewhere. But no blame would be heaped upon her for this. The circumstances were enough to cause anyone to want to find some other focus. It was simply a way of surviving, coping with something which she was unable to face directly.

Forcing herself back to reality she was faced by a sea of black shapes with their backs towards her. They were standing so she stood. At first she felt dizzy and was unable to recall why she was in this chilly, grey church. It was a funeral but for whom she could not remember. Why they had stood soon became clear as black-clad figures left the pews. They made for the front of the church and she followed.

They were filing around an open coffin to pay their last respects. She could not avoid this as she was caught in line. It brought back memories of standing above an open grave sprinkling soil on a casket; someone she loved. Still she could not recall who this was and she was nearing the front of the church and the open coffin. She gazed down and saw herself clad in black; then she was gazing at the roofing beams and a descending darkness as the lid was closed.

Nicola Grant

IT WAS THERE

The old house was in darkness. Its ancient hair raising hide away was inches from the hideous figure head that adorned the hallway!

Vincent Halliday had heard of the curse of the doomed pirate ship that lay at the bottom of the bay. Steps led up to the old house!

Treasure other than the load lost at the bottom of the bay was reported to be in the old house for generations.

Vincent decided it was now or never. So with several handy torches, he broke into the old house.

Vincent with his torch full on jumped when the other door creaked loudly in the silence of the hall. Swish! What is that screamed Vincent! He lost his torch, it went out!

With another torch in his hand, Vincent made for the staircase. He was quite sure he saw the eyes of one of the pictures move!

Beginning to get the jitters, Vincent took the creaking staircase two at a time. On the landing above a hand touched his shoulder! He turned and flashed his torch, it was a large cobweb, thick with dust. A door opened of its own accord along the landing. Looking down into the hall, he was staring at a gruesome face, its mouth opened and let out a terrifying yell!

Vincent ran towards the open door and fled in. Bang! The door shut!

'Another come for the lolly!'
Vincent made for the door.
'Too late, you're now standing on the traitor's trapdoor.'

Laughter! Gone! Shriek . . .

Alma Montgomery Frank

THE OLD RECTORY

Working on the top floor Sarah could hear the rectory grandfather clock chiming the midnight hour. Although her work hours were sometimes long she was happy in her new position. It was just the disembodied footsteps and creaking floorboards downstairs which disturbed her. She didn't say anything in case the rector disapproved.

Liz too, was happy working at the Old Rectory, except for the occasional creepy footsteps making the floorboards creak upstairs, but it was an old house and she was imaginative.

A howling storm buffeted the house making windows rattle. Liz, on the middle floor, checked everyone was settled, some of the residents didn't like storms. And then she heard the footsteps overhead. A wandering resident maybe? Liz didn't believe that and steeling herself she walked down the corridor towards the upper stairs.

Sarah, turning down her master's bed, heard the footsteps downstairs. Facing fear and praying quietly she picked up the oil lamp, crept downstairs and along the L-shaped corridor.

At the corridor's corner both girls came face to face and screamed. Liz turned and hurtled down the front staircase while Sarah dropped her lamp and flew down the back staircase. So great was her terror Sarah was unaware the floorboards were alight.

Simultaneously the girls ran into the drawing room shrieking they had seen a ghost but neither hearing the other.

In the hallway the grandfather clock, now two minutes slow after years of faithful service and surviving the fire of 1842, mournfully chimed the midnight hour.

Debbie McQuiston

DOCKINGDALE HALL

It was dark in the mansion house and Terry and I kept very quiet as we shone the torches up the winding staircase. In the first bedroom, there was a skeleton hanging on the wall and a painting of a fox. I looked out the window, Terry put his hand on my shoulder and I felt nervous. I looked into his brown eyes. 'What are we looking for?'
He shrugged his shoulders, 'We haven't come to steal anything, I'm just curious if there is a ghost.'

In the second bedroom Terry found a feather hat and shone the torch under his chin. He looked very scary. I thought, if somebody touches Terry on the shoulder now, he'll jump through the roof. Then to our surprise, a secret door opened next to the bookshelf. A tall thin lady dressed in white, held a lamp, she said, 'It's always the same when you're looking for something, you can never find it. Uncle George was never the one to throw things out.' She paused. 'I'm looking for a map.' She put the lamp on the chair and looked at Terry who stood with his mouth open. 'Have you come to help with the furniture removal?'
Terry shrugged his shoulders then looked at me quickly and we both ran out the room like frightened cats . . .

Kenneth Mood

HIS MAJESTY'S PLEASURE

In the dungeon of the stately castle, the air is sickly and fetid. Set into the wall there is a tiny, sunken chamber, a dungeon within a dungeon, called an 'oubliette'. The present occupant of this hellish pit has scarcely room to breathe, let alone move.

Employed as a gardener in the palace grounds, Will Day now suffers the consequences of daring to speak to the King's daughter. His innocent action deemed highly offensive, he is detained at His Majesty's Pleasure. Daily Will hears the anguished screams of fellow prisoners on the rack.

'God have mercy on our souls,' he prays fervently and cradles his head despairingly in his hands. Before he was incarcerated, Will learned that many a prisoner had been left to rot in the pit. Small comfort for a defenceless man.

Inhaling the stench from the rancid straw, Will eventually slips into an uneasy sleep, but wakes in the inky darkness of night as sharp incisors pierce his flesh. Heart hammering, Will encounters a hairy body and dashes it against the wall. Mind and body in agony, he hears only the rasping of his ragged breath.

A meagre diet pushed through the grid, Will remains in the pit for ten days, and when hauled out unceremoniously, he is unable to stand, his legs completely numb. He glances at his brutish jailer. 'Am I to be set free?' But then he sees the flash of steel and feels the blade across his neck. Will's suffering is over.

Ann Madge

ROUNDABOUT

Amy drove with unaccustomed recklessness through the orange light and onto the well-lit roundabout. Only the fact that she was tired and hungry persuaded her to take the short cut home.

Tony had laughed at her fears when she'd tried to express the evil that penetrated her mind in that particular area, blaming her vivid imagination. Amy, however, was convinced that the essence of heinous acts lingering from the past, waited to claim their next victim.

She shrugged off the impulse to turn her head, conscious that she carried an unwanted passenger.

By the time Amy had garaged her car the sensation of corruption was fading and she greeted Tony with a kiss, grateful for the warmth and comfort of their modern house. Her nose twitched appreciatively at the pleasant aroma emanating from the kitchen, and tossing her coat aside she joined Tony who was now dishing up their dinner.

A tingle of fear prickled the nape of her neck. She could no longer see the man she loved, but an alien being with huge staring eyes and blistered skin. Innate knowledge pierced her brain as her arm swooped for the carving knife and in one fluid movement pierced the skin of her victim and thrust into his flesh, leaving him no time to defend himself.

Tony dropped like a stone onto the tiled floor, blood pumping from the fatal wound. Amy fell to her knees, her tears raining down on the immobile face of her beloved husband.

Helen Mitchelhill

THE EBONY MASK

It was grotesque. A West African ebony mask with ivory teeth gazed down at her from the lounge wall. Jonathan, a lifelong friend, had given it to her as a combined birthday gift and souvenir from his latest globe-trotting adventure. Staring at it, she really wished he hadn't.

No matter where she was in the room, its hollow eyes followed her. It gave her the creeps and it was no good turning her back on it either because she could feel it watching her. Once or twice she'd turned round with a start thinking someone was standing right behind her but, of course, there was no one else in the room.

Unwavering, the mask stared back at her. It mesmerised her, seeming to come alive. Its eyes closing slowly then opening again. 'Ellen,' it whispered deeply, smiling at her. 'I have come for you.'

Her ears were filled with the sound of drum beats. The room echoed with voices singing, though the language was unfamiliar. She was suffocating. The temperature in the room was rising and she could hear flames crackling. The lights had gone out but the flickering of the flames sent shadows dancing on the walls. Her heart pounded. Then everything went black and she collapsed in a heap on the floor.

When she came round, she was alone, lying on the settee. The mask's hollow eyes fixed on her.

A man's shadow slid along the wall, stopping beneath the mask. She screamed. 'Ellen! It's me,' whispered Jonathan.

Kim Montia

REPAIRING THE GUTTERS

Am I alone? No, I can't be. That tapping sound . . . it's like a metronome . . . ticking . . . ticking . . . an implacable stopwatch, telling me, with every beat, that *he's* taken away another second of my life.

And the humming . . . a chorus of death. But where is it? I can hear it so clearly . . . it's practising, even now, for the ritual . . . they're preparing to feast on my soul . . . I can see their faces . . . their skin . . . white, stretched, bleached . . . like skulls . . . their bodies shrouded in dark cloaks . . .

And that howling . . . outside . . . *it* can't be human. It must be the Devil himself. Calling. He wants me. Now. Well, I'm *not* going to submit. Why should I make it easy for him. No. I shall stay here . . . lie here . . . I *won't* give in . . .

Oh, God, that's *him*, on the roof . . . yes, he's scratching, scrabbling, clattering on the tiles. He's getting nearer . . . now he's tapping on the window. Those must be his fingers, fluttering . . . no, they're claws . . . beating softly against the glass. Go away! . . . I *won't* let you in . . .

How did he *get* in? He's in the house . . . how *could* he get in? That creak . . . he's coming up the stairs. He's coming for me . . . he'll be in my *room* in a moment. Oh, God . . . please . . . *please* go away . . . I'm not *ready* for you yet . . .

Nick Brigham

FAUST AND FOR MOST

The house was old, creepy-old, and hard to heat. Crouching atop a rugged hill, the low-wattage bulbs in the only two rooms used gleamed malevolently, like the eyes of some misshapen cat observing every move of an unwary prey. The townspeople pursued their mundane existence, only occasionally bestowing a passing glance upon the house hundreds of feet above.

With a scowl, the swarthy unshaven writer crumpled the last rejection letter into a tight ball and hurled it into the far corner of the room. He had seen for himself the 'gems of literature', which scooped the major prizes and found them mediocre.

For a long time he had convinced himself that this was merely a case of sour grapes, but recently - in the smaller writers' magazines - he had detected a growing disillusionment amongst the better poets and authors.

He had been right all along; now he had nothing to lose by consulting *that* book. He arose from his creaky chair, stretched his back and yawned - sucking in air uncharacteristically frigid. He gasped at its invigorating touch, an electric pulse which urged him onward, upward beyond the rickety staircase towards the dusty, cobwebby bookshelf.

The book slid out easily from between its companions, opening at the very page he had read all those years ago. The strange figures on the page he knew were runes of vengeful misfortune, irreversible, irrevocable.

He had his story, but his conscience bothered him.

Still he submitted it!

Perry McDaid

SLIMMER'S DREAM

I had this simply wonderful dream, everything I ate made me slimmer! Chocolates, puddings, pies - the avoirdupois just faded away and so did I. Rings fell off, jeans magically enlarged - nothing fitted - I was positively bony. Salt-cellars huge, jaw razor-sharp. Friends vanished too, they couldn't cope. A nightmare indeed and then I awoke and found it was true . . .

Eileen M Lodge

GRAFFITI

Flickering firelight played upon the cave wall throwing fleeting shadows across a million year old canvas of glittering crystalline quartz. Deep inside the Earth Mother's womb three figures also cast their own, naked shades upon the living rock - two kneeling, heads bowed and silent, the third intoning and entranced, swaying gently from foot to foot.

Above them the smoke vanished into pitch-black cavernous heights, rising sparks lost forever in a night of elemental fear and wonder, whilst outside, oblivious to their rituals, wolf and wildcat fought and spat with an endless, feral hatred.

It was an old and dark time, a time for cruel mysticism and for cold preparation. The herds of deer and auroch would soon be treading their star-driven migratory ways, and the hunters must be given heightened powers to ensure a rich and bloody harvest.

Deft strokes of chewed ash-root left black and yellow representations of man and beast in bold outline. Here an arrow pierced a stag's neck, there two huntsmen speared a huge wild bull as red ochre blood spilled freely from fatal wounds. The artist's supple fingers traced a vicious scene of butchery as the incantations reached a shrieking climax.

Then, suddenly, it was over.

She cast the painting-root into the fire and placed her hands upon the bowed heads of the two sweating men. Her bearskin head-dress shook as she laughed silently, confident in her power. High above her savage world the twin horns of a new moon pierced the gathering darkness.

Alan Hodgson

FORCES OF EVIL

I used to live in a small village in Russia. The most haunted village on earth, as it would later come to be known. And it was from here that my grandfather would tell me tales that turned my stomach and chilled my blood. He told me that in his time, an ominous dark force had swept the great 'Mother Land' like a raging whirlwind. And the evil that was contained within that whirlwind would stain every Russian life with the innocent blood of millions.

It had begun when an insane demon in a far away land unleashed his crazed minions. He, my grandfather went on, ordered those minions to drench the Steppes in our blood. He would brainwash his frenzied followers into believing that they were doing the right thing and merely carrying out God's Holy Law. He said that all the 'sub-humans' that inhabited the Red Kingdom had to be permanently eradicated. No mercy was to be shown to anyone. Bodies could be burnt, raped, shot or simply starved to death. It would become a horror story of epic proportions.

But our people fought the demon on his own terms. We pushed his grey hoard all the way back from wence they had came. And when we finally cornered the rabid beast, he simply cowered in his lair and ended his life.

The name of my haunted village is called Chernobyl. And, as I will never have grandchildren of my own. Please tell my grandfather's tale to everybody else.

Michael Bellerby

THE CATACOMBS

It was dark, damp and cold. The wall I was against was of rough stone and for the life of me I couldn't remember where I was. Stumbling to my feet I groped along as far as it went. Suddenly it disappeared. I walked forward a few steps until my nose hit another wall.

I decided to go to my left. I continued. The wall abruptly stopped and turned right. I thought to myself, this is strange. If only I had looked around before walking along the wall I might have seen the way out.

Following the wall to the right, I found some hollows cut into the wall about four feet square. My hand slipped into one.

It touched something cold and I pulled it out suppressing a scream. What in God's name have I gotten into, I thought. I saw a light up ahead and I decided to go that way. Big mistake!

As I neared the light, I heard voices but couldn't make them out. As I got closer still, the voices became clearer. They were chanting something, but I couldn't make it out.

I continued forward and tripped over a raised piece of stone. I fell forward and banged my head. I felt around and to my amazement I felt steps. I climbed them only to find a locked door. I hammered on the door and to my relief I heard the lock click.

I let out a terrified scream before I fainted.

Dennis Barrasin

THE HAND PRINTS

At last the day arrived. They had saved for years for a safari holiday and they were about to set off across the desert in ten fully loaded 4x4s.

Fifty miles were covered before reaching the first stops at an oasis. That night a sandstorm blew in, wrecking the tents and burying most of the 4x4s. Next morning the Richardson's noticed that their only child was missing; they had been advised their little one would not be in danger.

Helped by a wandering tribe of nomads, in vain they searched the desert for hours.

The nomads told them the desert seldom gave up its dead, they should accept their loss and return home.

At home, the grieving mother sought the help of the finest medium in the country and soon the whole family sat around her table.

Once in a trance, the medium started to speak in the voice of her spirit guide, Lone Wolf, a Red Indian Chief, who said he knew the child and would fetch him.

Suddenly, after a long silence, everybody took fright on hearing the voice of a child calling out 'Mother, Father, are you there? Please answer if you're there.'

The little boy's grandfather stood up and turned on the light. From under his feet came a gritty crunching sound.

All assembled saw to their astonishment that, around the backs of their chairs was a layer of sand, scuffed with the tracks of dragging knees and the imprints of tiny hands.

D P Bardoe

FRIGHTMARE

All alone in a large house or cottage, in a town or on a desolate moor, why did we watch those old movies of ghouls and ghosts and gore. At length when the film had ended, and the picture had faded and gone, there was nothing but the sound, that high pitched sound, that droned on and on.

You got up from your seat to switch off the set, but the horror stayed in your mind and you could not forget. Though sleep called you could not retire, so you settled back into your seat to gaze at the fire. In silence you sat, you're all alone, and as weariness overtook you your thoughts they did roam. With thoughts of that night, your mind it did sway, and soon your subconscious would suck you away.

Was that the sound of footsteps, of heavy feet, that echoed in your brain as your heart skipped a beat? A creak on the staircase, the rush of wind against the door. The phone rang, but no one answered, could you bear any more?

Were you really alone, was there anybody there, as you felt that brush of deathly cold air?

Even today, when we are weary the mind plays its tricks. So sleep the deep sleep, as the broken clock ticks.

A S McKay

To The Depths

Sarah worked in a towering new building in the city, and hated it. Her job as a PA was fine, but she detested the place itself. Something there got on her nerves. Things were always going wrong - lifts suddenly ceased operating, lights failed. Someone once remarked grimly that it was constructed on top of an old plague burial pit.

Sarah finished work very late one night. Everyone had gone, even cleaners. The building was profoundly silent, cold, lights flickering again. She then discovered the lifts were out of action, meaning a long descent from the twentieth floor. Once before, she had felt she would never reach ground level. Now she looked again at the flight of stairs winding below. She decided to count as she walked.

It was icy, increasingly dark - nineteenth floor . . . seventeenth . . . fourteenth . . . seemingly endless . . . eleventh . . . tenth . . . half-way! She stumbled, grabbing the handrail. The last thing she needed was to fall headfirst. Eighth . . . sixth . . . third . . . and finally - ground floor.

Then an unexpected problem. She peered around - no exit door into the lobby. She couldn't get out. She must continue further downwards to the basement/car park, leaving that way.

The stairs now led into greater blackness, but she thought she could hear voices. So she ventured on, counting steps, which seemed ever steeper . . . one . . . two . . . fifty . . . ninety . . . two hundred . . . three . . . and still lower, for there was no escape back up, just that relentless forward pull.

Sarah reached two thousand - and now the voices were counting with her.

Daphne Stroud

IN THE SHADOWS

As she opened the door to the cellar, cold, musty air hit her face. Sam shuddered while holding the torch in front of her. I wish Colin had replaced the bulb which blew last week, she thought as she descended into the shadowy depths. A loud bang, wind had blown the door shut, she was imprisoned in the cellar.

If only her mother would wait until daylight to find the box, but she was impatient as ever. What was that? Something crept in the shadows, 'Get off, get off, oh! It's only a spider,' Sam noticed the enormous cobweb hanging from the ceiling.

Trying to erase images of spiders and various insects, Sam felt her way further into the darkest corners of the room. 'God, hope the battery lasts,' glad of the torch to hold. 'Oh blast,' she said, as she stubbed her toe on a jutting piece of hardboard. 'Really must clear this out tomorrow.' Slowly she advanced, praying she could find the precious box.

She heard a long eerie groan, then another. 'Silly me, it's the wind, where the hell is that box?' Then Sam heard a movement, as her torch began to flicker she heard it again. Peering deep into the dark, she saw him staring at her. With the final beam of light, before the torch died she saw the gun, it was pointing straight at her.

S Mullinger

THE CUPBOARD OF FEAR

Midnight, and he, at fourteen, was all alone in this ancient house where it was reputed a gruesome murder had been committed in years gone by. Wind howled through the trees outside, their twigs rattling along the slate roof above him. The fire had burnt low, cinders tinkling in the grate. The grandfather clock continued to tick with ponderous regularity.

But soon a different sound came creeping in.

Drip! Drip! Drip! Drip!

He listened. There it was again! He knew it wasn't the water tap. No tap was in the room. He stood still, terror gripping him. If only he could stop trembling and go and investigate from where this sound was coming. His glance shifted to a huge cupboard in the corner where dark shadows were cast by a flickering oil lamp. 'Cupboard big enough,' ran his fevered thoughts, 'to hide a body in.'

Drip . . . Drip . . . Drip . . .

The tempo had slowed down somewhat. Maybe the noise was coming from the cupboard? Gingerly, he approached it, and touched the gooey liquid which was seeping out from under the door.

'It's blood!' Panic stricken, he yelled aloud, as with loathing he viewed the sticky mess. He turned the knob. Slowly the door opened. What revolting sight was revealed as he looked inside the cupboard?

A dismembered corpse? A gory human head?

Hysterical laughter now shook him back into relieved normality.

Who earlier, at supper time, had accidentally knocked over a large bottle of tomato sauce?

Loré Föst

THE VISITOR

At last Rebecca had arrived. She couldn't remember the last time she was here and stood looking around the room, and noticed the old clock on the mantelpiece had stopped, but there was still a familiarity about it, the fireplace was still the same and the flames flickered in the gloom, casting shadows on the walls.

It was getting late, feeling rather tired, sat in the chair nearest the fire, bringing comfort, everything seemed idyllic, her fingers twiddled with the lace collar on her fine linen dress. Rebecca felt as if she was waiting, but for what, and couldn't understand this feeling of expectation, then waived the idea out of her head. 'I'm just being silly,' she thought, gave a sigh and looked around properly for the first time since arriving.

Rebecca became aware, not so much of the room, but the atmosphere around her.

It was getting dark outside and the ivy was tapping intermittently on the window, shadows from the flames danced over the walls giving a more eerie foreboding, the air becoming more stifled.

The moon began to shine through the window, giving little relief to the room inside. Slowly Rebecca went to the window and peered outside, she could hear the sound of hooves getting closer, then silence.

The outline of the rider moved towards the house, cold terror embraced her, the door flew open. Fainting, he caught her before she fell, then they both dissolved into the night.

The clock started ticking again . . .

Eileen Jones

THE JOURNEY

He felt pleased that he had ended their affair for the guilt had overwhelmed him, replacing the initial excitement. He had no intention of letting his wife down again just for the sake of his middle-aged ego flattered by the attentions of a woman young enough to be his daughter.

The night was vile: rain lashed down from a black sky and the wind howled a dissonant tune as he drove home. He had stopped off at a pub after telling her it was over. He knew it was the right thing to do but it had upset him deeply to see her begging him not to leave. The beer had slipped down very easily and he was undoubtedly drunk, his mind far away from the dangers of the road.

He just did not see them as he raced down the dark country lane. All he heard was a sickening thud as his car impacted with a woman. A selfish impulse made him carry on but then he found that his conscience forced him to stop. In an instance he was sober and vomited by the side of the road.

He went back on the worst trip of his life. A man was cradling a woman in his arms. To his horror he saw the woman was his wife and obviously dead.

'You did it deliberately,' cried an injured man, voice a mixture of pain and grief, 'you knew we were having an affair, you bastard.'

Guy Fletcher

KITTY

It was dark and dismal, a thickly overcast night as Kitty patrolled her domain. This was her alleyway and she knew every brick, every cracked slab that adorned its length.

Stealthily she crept along its black, damp, boundary wall, her eyes glowing a venomous green as she scanned the path below. Suddenly she froze as if a statuette, for out of the corner of her eye she sensed movement.

There, down there amongst a trio of trash cans she saw them.

Nimbly she leapt down and slowly inched closer, barely perceptible to the naked eye as she hugged the shadows.

Her senses tingled, electrically alive with anticipation as she intently focused upon her prey.

They would pay dearly for this trespass. Up ahead the scampering of tiny feet could now be heard as her prey delved hungrily amidst the trash.

On hearing this, Kitty quickened her pace as she prepared to spring into action. Full pelt she raced across the pathway. Her prey halting as one glanced towards her, but wait, something was wrong.

 For instead of scattering away in terror, they turned enmasse and leapt upon her, ripping and tearing at her flesh. Biting down deep into the sweet succulent meat, warm blood dribbling from their snarling jaws. They squealed with delight as poor Kitty screechs out her anguish as her little feline body is ravenously torn apart by the pack of starving rats she foolishly mistook for easy prey.

P N Dawson

RETRIBUTION

Dark, angry clouds touched the horizon, lurid flashes of lightning lit the sea with an eerie glow. Thunder crashed, grew louder as the storm raced towards her, raging with untamed might.

She watched the sea as it smashed against the rocks far below, each wave bigger than the one before. She felt at one with nature, enjoying the turbulent emotions as the icy wind rushed up the cliff and encircled her in its violent embrace. As driving rain stung her face, she flung her arms wide, intoning incantations stolen from her father's book.

He had forbidden her ever to open it, or indeed, to enter his room, but she had taken the key whilst he slept and with fast beating heart, had unlocked the door, found the book and with trembling hand, had copied the spell she sought. The candle flickered and an unearthly sound filled the room as she hurried to lock the door and return the key before he woke.

Her voice rose with the wind, shrieking, her words no longer audible. Before long, she was aware of a change in the clouds, a form was taking shape, constantly distorting, it writhed, until suddenly becoming dreadfully clear to her. This was the Devil himself, horns, hooves, and eyes so malevolent, she could not look away.

Too late, she realised she had not spoken the last vital words of the spell. Utter terror overcame her as the Devil claimed his own.

A Odger

DEVIL'S BEGINNING

The silence of the night, black and eerie with the occasional hoot from an owl. I had wandered in the waves of sleep and was overcome by the night and the strangest feeling that I was waiting for someone, or something! I wasn't disappointed for a cloak of black stood before me urging me forward, I could smell my own fear, taste my own blood as I bit hard on my lower lip.

Taking the bony hand of the black cloak, I was led into a coven of lighted candles and people swathed in robes. I feared the worst and was led to the alter of Satan where the Devil in scarlet mumbled magic words to his chanting audience. I lay on the stone so cold and watched the flickering candles and felt the cold steel of the Devil's instrument. As a gust of wind blew a candle over, my flimsy gown was soon afire.

Suddenly I was awake and I ran and ran, the chill of the night air as I rolled in the ground spread over my body, and I found the strength to run. I took the police and friends to the coven the next night only to find an empty cave with cobwebs and blackness. On the way out I stumbled and the end of a large candle held my gaze. Was it the end or was it the Devil's beginning?

Elizabeth Corr

QUILLO

Quillo's all-seeing eyes were no enemy of the dark. He knew every inch of the wood, and the slightest footfall was like thunder in his ears. Quillo was a true predator.

From up high in the larch, he sat as if on a royal throne, his head twisting this way and that, listening intently for the sign that would satisfy his hunger. Suddenly, he spotted his prey. It looked frightened, as if it were an alien in this strange land, and, looking up, it saw Quillo ready to pounce. She shrieked a little, yet in pleasant anticipation. They had made their rendezvous, as arranged.

A glint of metal reflected itself against the moon. Quillo smelt blood. His prey slumped to the ground, a lesson taught for lies and deceit. Quillo made his escape, the darkness folding protectively over him.

His great grandfather, Antonio Quillo, nicknamed 'Birdman of Verona', for his flight-like agility, was executed many years before, for a similar crime. 'It's all in the genes' thought Quillo as he scaled a beech tree for the night. 'I can't help it.'

Janice Turner

TWO FINGERS OF WHISKY

The party had been brilliant. Driving home afterwards I was glad I had not had any alcohol as the fog swirled and visibility was pretty poor. The unlit windy roads back to town were lined with hedges which took on ghostly shapes.

I was tense by the time the lights of town finally came into sight as I slowly drove round the coast road so I did not resent it when the first traffic lights I came to were at red. In fact I put on the hand brake and closed my eyes to relax for a second.

Suddenly and without warning there was a crash on the windscreen. The scream caught in my throat. A hulking shape of a man was standing in front of my car wielding a thick chain. The first blow had hit the windscreen which had shattered in the way they do. He hit the side of the car. Fortunately the main force hit the door just below the window which was inches from my head.

They call it the fight - flight reaction: in this case flight was the answer and I drove. The lights were still red and the chain maniac in front. I drove round him, onto the pavement. Nothing was coming along the other road.

When I got home I checked my car. The chain had caught on the boot handle. It was still wrapped round two of my attacker's fingers.

Inside I drank two fingers of whisky.

Keith F Lainton

THIRTEEN

He praised himself. Six months of arduous training at dawn had paid off. Without a doubt, today was to be a day of triumph. The thought of fulfilling an ambition sent a rush of adrenaline throughout his numb limbs. To his surprise, the thrill of taking part in a full marathon was more satisfying than a night of red-hot passion. As for bearing thirteen on his T-shirt: well, superstitious doom seemed to enhance his performance. Unlucky? No, just pessimistic nonsense!

As he reached the home straight, his breathing became more laboured. However, cheers from the far-flung crowd willed him to drive onwards, to the site of the finish. The physical and mental pain now contorted his pale face. His legs buckled with spasms and fatigue. Overwhelmed by the crowds' response, he drew on reserves of pride, and fought to lengthen his stride.

His chest tightened. His lungs burnt with the fierce strain. Now desperate, he drew deeper breaths. His heart pounded, almost to the point of exploding. Fearless, he continued. Then, with one final push, he thrust his blistered frame over the line. The crowd fell silent; scenes of euphoria had transformed to scenes of sheer terror. Trembling with dire exhaustion, he heaved himself off the soiled tarmac. His attention was drawn to a group of paramedics; they were frantically trying to revive a blurred figure. Then it dawned on him that the fatality was wearing thirteen. He had witnessed his own death.

Sandra Edwards

THE SCARECROW

It came to the field by the lane. The scarecrow.

No one knew how or why - it just appeared one dark - windy - Hallowe'en night.

The farmer was puzzled - but praised his luck - and moved it to the centre - but next morning it was back in the exact spot on the edge of the field by the gate - in a six foot radius around the spot where the farmer had moved it - nothing ever grew again.

The cut of the coat and hat - spoke of days long gone - and even on the warmest day the cloth felt wet and moist - that is to those brave enough to feel it - every Friday blood ran down the shoulder and sleeve - never once forming a pool on the ground - only one man touched that blood - his screams were heard two miles away in the village - as he ran down the lane waving a withered talon - that once was his hand.

No one dared walk down that lane on Hallowe'en - the sounds of battle - the clash of sabres - and the screaming of tormented souls chilled the blood of the strongest and bravest - it came to the field that scarecrow - to - scareman - forever.

Norbert Atherton

STONE COLD

A kestrel hovered in the sky above the hill where a monument pointed like a huge, concrete needle towards the sun. There was nobody around but the young couple on the hill, he seated on the stone steps at the foot of the monument, and she standing a short distance away.

The young man had a guitar. He strummed pensively, staring down at his feet, a cigarette tucked behind his ear. Now and again he would look up at the woman who stood with her back to him, gazing into the distance, her snake-like dreadlocks streaming in the wind.

The wind was strong now. A sudden gust blew the cigarette out from the young man's ear. The woman, who had turned towards him, stooped to pick it up, and as she looked up to hand it to him, their eyes met.

Suddenly the young man found himself unable to move. His heart seemed to stop beating, and he felt a chill inside as if his innards were turning as cold as the stone he sat on.

With horror he realised what was happening. He tried to get away but he couldn't move, nor even turn his head to avoid her gaze. The chill had spread to his neck now. It felt like cold fingers closing around his throat, and all the while her eyes were looking into his.

At length Medusa turned away, and, with a flick of her serpentine dreadlocks, she walked off, leaving the statue behind her.

Sonia Watts

THE CRUCIFIX

It was midnight, and in the car's headlights I saw the glaring eyes of a wolf-like creature. I had to slow down, as it was in the middle of the road, and seemed to stare me in the eyes and dare me to get closer. I swerved onto the verge and carried on, thinking to myself that although I'd had a few drinks, I hadn't imagined it all.

I was tired and just lay on the bed without undressing, still thinking of the animal, and how it had looked at me. I was awakened by the light of the full moon shining on me through the open window. I was hot and sweaty and my face felt swollen, rushing to the mirror, I was horrified to find my face had turned into a face of a wolf.

Something seemed to take control of me, for I jumped onto the window sill and gave a mighty howl, before running along the shadowy streets, frightening the few people I met. I had sense enough to realise that I needed help, so I made for a local convent. On entering I saw a nun kneeling before a cross.

She wasn't shocked when I told her my story, she merely placed her crucifix around my neck and told me to go back home to bed. Next morning I woke up thinking it was just a bad dream, until I looked in the mirror, still hanging around my neck was the crucifix.

Keith Coleman

MERTHYR MANSIONS

Why was she staying? Didn't think I'd steal anything surely? There was nothing *to* steal. Everything was as I'd left it. Even the chair in which I'd been sitting on that fateful day when . . . oh why did she keep hanging around? I wasn't there to rummage through things. Just to see if it were still there - the figure on the balcony across the park. Always in three-quarter profile, never turning its head so I could see whether it were man or woman, never eating or drinking, reading or knitting. Just there whenever I looked up, taunting me, obsessing me.

How it had overshadowed my life - like a monstrous bird from some horror-haunted world, forever fanning me down, down . . . That's why I had to come back - back to where it all began. I had to . . .

'If you're looking for Merthyr Mansions you won't find it.'
I started. How did she know I was looking for Merthyr Mansions? I didn't know myself I was looking for Merthyr Mansions.

'Murder Mansions the tabloids called it. Twenty skeletons they found there - behind walls, under floorboards.'

I looked round. She was still by the door, her face averted, staring, it seemed, into nothingness. Her hands, which I'd never been able to see because they'd been below the level of the balcony, were tense and prehensile like claws. But it was her head. Her head. That same amorphous, phantasmic, mock-human head. I gasped. She turned towards me. Smiling.

Sarah Knox

RE-UNITED

The old lady closed her eyes. Still, behind closed lids, she could see the figures surrounding her. They were nameless, faceless creatures - appearing to float, suspended in nothingness.

The room was bare but for the torn mattress on which she lay. A battered clock ticked monotonously - echoing through the silence. Somewhere in her mind she could hear the sound. 'Tick-tock' - or was it her own heartbeat - knelling the seconds left to her?

Slowly she opened her eyes. The figures were still there, hanging around her like muslin drapes.

The old lady knew she was dying. Death seemed a long time in coming - not the thief in the night she had always imagined.

Suddenly the figures were moving, caressing her with distorted ghostly limbs, pulling at her body, her vision, her soul. Who were they, she silently mused . . . there had been so many she had lost count. Their names, their lives, their faces were sealed in another time, another place.

Her body felt weightless, like a wind-tossed feather which would never land. The clock stopped! Heralding another, more sinister arrival.

The figures were all over her now, inside her - their mass indistinguishable as separate entities, they were one - they were death.

She knew death.

Death had been her reason to live. An ironic half-smile creased her face. One by one her victims whispered their names in her ear as they lifted her up to join them - united in death as never in life.

Elaine Campbell

JUNGLE!

'Wait here,' said Joe to the other two. 'I'll try to stop someone on the road. It's only half a mile.'

'But quick!' said Elise. 'I think my leg is broken . . . and I don't like it here!'

'Do you want some water?' asked Rick of his sister, watching the experienced Joe disappear along the jungle track.

'No, help!' she snapped. 'Been ill-fated, this back-pack holiday . . . what's that?'

Rick turned smartly. The small fire was crackling, and he suggested the noise was sourced there. His hand, nevertheless, discreetly found the machete. The pair's wits were on alert. The moment passed.

Elise drank thirstily, her throat dry. 'Sip!' commanded Rick, concerned at their water shortage.

'I'll damn well drink it all!' she retorted, frustrated, petulantly hurling the canteen deep into the undergrowth.

'Now there's no water,' exclaimed Rick. 'Unless I find it!' He set off, and Elise complained. 'It's only over there,' he said, and was half way towards it, when a small stone hit his sister on the chest.

'Rick!' she screamed. Her brother's abdomen was already slashed open, from chest to groin. He never saw or heard the attack; but felt the numbing agony, an instant before his mortality expired. Elise felt vulnerable, and cried out again, and again.

It heard the calls with naked ears; and with black eyes, looked down on its second victim. Elise did not realise she was already dead.

S Pete Robson

THE VERY LAST CUP OF TEA

He gingerly placed the gravy boat on the tray beside the little green jug. 'I believe it is the one she used to put flowers in - stood on the mantelpiece,' he said to himself. 'When was that? Last week? Week before? She was well then, anyway it was long before we ran out of milk. Lucky I found these whiteners - what airline was it? Funny how you forget these things.' He stirred the liquid in the gravy boat.

He manoeuvred the tray onto the black japanned little trolley - used to stand in the porch with plants on. He put them outside the window to catch the rain. One day soon he'd take them down the garden.

He turned the trolley around because the front wheels came off yesterday when he tripped, and pushed the trolley into the wall of the passage - scraped the paper - must see to that. So much to do and it was so difficult without his spectacles. They were somewhere on the stairs. When he fell he remembered seeing them bounce in front of him.

He was going to pick them up, but his hand flopped around so. Opened his shirt and put his right hand inside. Didn't hurt now and his leg had stopped throbbing, the swelling had turned black, but he could put his weight on it without the shoe - seemed quite good. Funny smell when he touched it, I must bathe it in hot water. Later, not now, must take the tea up to Molly.

He leaned against the trolley and steered with one hand. The front wheels which were now the back, dragged along the carpet, so he had to lift it. His foot caught in some broken crockery and he stumbled to his knees. A sharp point stabbed into his leg. He gasped with pain - reached down with his hand - came away red - wiped the blood into the carpet and got to his feet. That foot was hurting again.

He sat on the bottom stair and closed his eyes for a moment. The tray was slipping off the trolley. Somehow he balanced it and fumbled for the stair lift.

By the time he got the seat down and sat on it with the tray off the trolley and on his lap, the little green jug was gone.

Never mind, it was for him. He'd say he's had his downstairs! He pushed the button and the lift started with a jerk. The gravy boat split a drop of liquid on his bleeding leg. He didn't realise it had been cold a long time.

At the top of the stairs he fell forward out of the chair lift and banged his head on the newel post. He thought he sat on the landing carpet for some time. The gravy boat was on its side, there was a drop or two in the bottom, maybe more. He hoped she wouldn't be very thirsty.

On hands and knees he pushed at the door and shuffled into the room on his bottom. Her hand was hanging down and he put the gravy boat on the floor and forced himself - on his good leg - onto the bed, then reached down and caught hold of the vessel.

'It's just a drop of tea.' He dribbled a drop onto her lips that were slightly parted as they had been since she died a week ago.

Peter E Smith

THE CELLAR

Tom hesitated as he opened the cellar door, gazing down the damp steps into the impenetrable gloom. Since his wife Sally died six months ago, he had not been down, being claustrophobic didn't help.

His torch flickered into life, propping the door open was an old habit. The thought of being shut in down there made him jump, all his life he avoided confined spaces, never comfortable without a door, window or natural light.

As he stepped down, the darkness seemed to engulf him. Then the steps seemed to take an eternity, from the bottom, the open door looked miles away. Quickly he hurried back, nearing the top, his foot slipped on the damp step. Trying to save himself, he dislodged the prop. The door slammed shut and Tom tumbled down the stairs, dropping his torch. Terror gripped him immediately, his heartbeat rapidly increasing. He felt the panic rising and pain began to burn in his chest. Sobbing with fear his hand struck the torch, now sweating profusely imagination began to run wild, just enough light to see an old deck chair, but surely another figure holding out a hand.

Pain suddenly so severe, breathing became impossible, Tom died instantly.

Neighbours and police found him some days later, his body by an old deck chair. Sally had obviously been dead some time, but the cold, dank cellar could not disguise the fact that she had been strangled.

T G Bloodworth

THE DOOR

The room was large with a ceiling that seemed to go up forever, topped off with a large striplight which flickered every few seconds like it was trying to send a message in Morse code.

James sat on a chair in the corner of the room, daring not to move in case he was spotted. What foul blow had fate dealt him this morning? Only God held that answer and even he was not telling this time.

Outside too seemed strangely quiet, with a sky slate grey and all too overbearing. All of this was pressure that was telling on James' stone face, which glistened with cold sweat. His eyes too were gripped with mortal fear, especially when he turned his gaze back to the door on the opposite side of the room. A large, heavy Victorian door, with a brass doorknob. From behind the door came a low humming noise, which was sending his brain swimming with terror. All too soon he would have to cross this unearthly threshold, and face the terror that lay beyond. As quick as the humming started, it stopped! Leaving the room in silence, except for the sound of footsteps walking across the adjacent room, towards the door.

Ever so slowly the doorknob began to turn, the heavy door swung open, to reveal a figure of a middle-aged woman, who entered the room and turned to face James. The breath seemed to stick in his throat as the woman looked at him and said in a quiet but terrifying voice, 'The dentist will see you now Mr Smith!'

Andy Whitfield

THE LIGHTHOUSE

The stones crunched beneath their feet making an ugly sound, as though the stones along the beach were willing them to stay away, to turn back. The darkness around them was suffocating.

Alison held tightly onto Jack's hand. This was supposed to be a romantic moonlit walk, but she was filled with an uneasy, fearful feeling. The moon cowered behind a huge cloud, plunging them into darkness.

The beach was spookily quiet, with only the occasional gentle splash of waves to break the silence.

Suddenly, a huge beam of light illuminated the waves, then the beach and finally Alison and Jack. While Alison was trying to cope with the shocking realisation that the beam had emerged from the long-deserted lighthouse, Jack seemed excited and eager to investigate.

'No, let's just go home Jack. I wouldn't feel safe, the place has been deserted for years.'
'All the more exciting,' Jack insisted. 'Just one quick look at the view, then we'll go home, I promise.'

Alison allowed herself to be pulled towards the lighthouse, all the time a fear growing heavy on her heart like a weight that could not be lifted. They climbed the spiral steps, all the while Jack assuring her of the incredible view at the top. Alison had stopped listening. She was too aware of the darkness, the cold, damp smell that filled the space around them.

Finally, they reached the top, and Alison gasped as she tried to take in the whole sight at once: the sea, the beach, and most of all, the stars. It was all so beautiful.

'At last,' sighed Jack snaking one arm around her waist. 'I've got you right where I want you.'

Confused, Alison turned to face him. A different gasp escaped from her mouth. A gasp of fear, of terror as she realised her husband was holding a gun.

'Don't scream.' Jack spoke quietly and calmly. 'Don't scream and don't run, not if you know what's good for you.'

Her eyes widened with horror and she began to run.

'You'll be sorry Alison,' Jack murmured.
Alison followed her instincts, and the path, to safety. She raced down the cold stone steps, two at a time. Ten to go, eight, six. As she ran, thoughts whirled around her mind, scrambled and distorted. In the distance she could hear the slow rhythm of following footsteps. She kept running. Only four steps to go. Two. She'd reached the bottom.

Her undying fear was her source of energy. Her legs moved with an automatic rhythm, and her breath was short and gasping. Just down the lane to their lonely home.

Suddenly, the situation hit her. This was her own husband. How could he be trying to kill her? Everything here was so familiar: the small fence around the garden that they had built together, the square lawn which they took turns to mow in the summer. How could this be happening?

She checked over her shoulder one last time then turned her key and stepped into safety.

'I told you not to run Alison.' Jack stood at the foot of the stairs, his evil stare fixed upon her.

Lucy Hammond (16)

THE LIGHTHOUSE

The lighthouse stood tall and alone in the darkness, a simple figure, straight and monumental. Charlie watched it from her bedroom window, the light turning round, showering the waves with flecks of silvery white as if it were paint on canvas. The sea fascinated Charlie.

It was almost midnight and the moon looked like a crystal ball floating in the sky, magical and exciting. The stars were hidden by the thick layer of cloud that blanketed the sky and a soft mist of frost was rolling over the sleeping flower beds like the waves from the ocean.

No matter how much she tried Charlie could not sleep. The outside was so inviting and comforting. Without a thought she opened her window and jumped out. The air seemed fresher somehow as if pollution had been cleared away by the sound of the crashing waves.

She wandered towards the cliffs and the lighthouse, pulling her coat around her to keep the frost out. The grass around her started to soak her shoes and her feet, her lips turned blue and in the moonlight she looked like a lost spirit roaming the land aimlessly.

Once at the lighthouse she looked around at the beautiful sea. She did not know why she had come but for tonight she felt that she belonged here. So there she stood, waiting. The waves were gently covering the sand and rocks then being pulled back to a clockwork rhythm. Charlie's mind wandered through the mystery of the ocean as she contemplated the wave formations. She leaned against the lighthouse wall and sighed.

Suddenly a noise interrupted her thoughts. A man's cough! She did not know whether to turn around and alert the man to her knowledge of his presence or to ignore it and hope that he had not seen her. Slowly she turned around to see a huge muscular giant standing maybe a yard behind her. She tried to scream but all that was heard was a small squeak slightly resembling a human sound. The man took a step closer and Charlie could see his face. It was old and weathered but his eyes sparkled in the moonlight. For a moment Charlie could see the deep ocean reflected in his eyes as the lighthouse beam once again swung across the sea. She knew he was what she was waiting for.

In a gentle voice, not fitting his appearance, he whispered: 'You yearn for something you do not believe exists. The knowledge of magic and truth and the power to control it.'

She did not understand this cryptic message but curiosity filled her heart and her mind begged for an answer. With no fear, Charlie's head motioned a single nod of acceptance.

The man closed his eyes in concentration and pointed towards the sea. Charlie looked, scanning the ocean for any change.

Nothing. Just open sea stretching for miles around.

Then the clouds began to blacken and the sea grew angry. Thunder and lightning were perfectly synchronised around her. The wind wailed in pain, the noise almost deafened her. The man just looked on as if he commanded the storm. Charlie did not know whether to run or stay.

'I surrender to you the knowledge and power of the universe!' he shouted. A collection of leaves swirled in the wind. As they flew over him, the man disintegrated as if he was dust blown off a book. Charlie could feel her heart beat throughout her body. She was numb with fear as the wind, containing the man's body or soul, she did not know which, came towards her.

She let out a scream as the wind encircled her; passing through her; giving her power; answering her questions.

Silence. No wind. No waves. No sound. Everything was waiting anxiously for her like soldiers waiting for their commander. Charlie lay on the ground; her eyes open; her mind conscious but her body was still numb.

Slowly her body began to move and the sea began to splash against the rocks and the leaves on the nearby trees rustled in the wind.

Kathy Eaton (16)

BEING FOLLOWED HOME

'Why, oh why must the bus stop be so far from home?'

Sally stumbled onto the kerb and stood as the bus droned slowly away into the fog. No chance of going by the short cut tonight, she thought, without street lighting it's doubtful, if I would ever make it. I wonder if it's true you just walk in circles?

She slowly made her way along the pavement leaving the friendly glow of the newsagent's window behind.

As she approached the corner, the influence of a comforting street lamp gradually became apparent, she headed towards it.

Somewhere behind her she detected a muffled footfall, slow, purposeful steps lost in the darkness.

Another poor soul picking his or her way home on this filthy night, she thought.

The orange glow of the street lamp hardly penetrated the dense gloom as she paused for a moment, ears straining for approaching traffic, before crossing.

That's strange, she thought, the footsteps have stopped, perhaps whoever it was has reached home. Lucky things.

Pulling her thick muffler closer she ventured on to the road, the footsteps resumed their measured tread, almost as though they were following. Once on the other side she paused, the footsteps stopped.

Suddenly she became aware of the cold and began to shiver. Must get home, she thought, I must get home as soon as possible, and with this simple thought in mind she headed towards the Avenue. Her steps quickened as she approached the pillar box on the corner. 'Should I ring for help at the nearby telephone kiosk? No once inside I'll be trapped and alone, better keep going.' By now she was at a jogging pace, her breath issuing as a white vapour in the cold air, all the time she was conscious of the following footsteps now becoming more rapid.

Her heart thumped as she accelerated, by now she was running, passing through the brighter zones of the street lamps and the darker voids between.

She reached the Crescent panting, her leaden feet labouring over the wet pavement, driven on by her own terror, lungs pumping and temples throbbing.

The light, at last, the light of the bay window glowing through the smoke of the night. Without breaking step she flung open the gate and leaped up the shadowy steps, wildly her fists pounded the door with what little strength she had left.

Open up. My God open up, her tortured mind screamed, though her quivering lips were unable to mouth the words. The door was wrenched open in answer to her urgency and she pitched forward, headlong into the hall.

'Sally, Sally,' cried her startled mother, 'whatever is the matter?' The collapsed heap at the bottom of the stairs gabbled incoherently and pointed a trembling hand towards the open door. The grey head switched round towards the street.

'There's no one out there,' she said, 'only that nice Mr Willoughby from number twelve, and he's in a tearing hurry to get home out of this dreadful fog.'

Janet Cavill

AFRICAN SAFARI

Do stop Dear. Look, pull over there. We'll watch the animals from
there.
(Bitch)

Wish we could get closer. Where's my camera? Love your aftershave.
Present from Gladys? Called Buffalo?
(Bitch)

Whe're my contacts? D'you like my dress? Gladys loaned me a safari
hat *and* one of her outfits. I bought a spray of elephant scent; Do so love
elephants.
(You look like one: bitch)

Gladys says elephant spray'll get you a man quicker'n you can stand up.
If Gladys had you Dear, she wouldn't need elephant spray; Dear.
(Elephant-bitch)

What's that noise Dear? Elephant? Quite sure? Not tiger or lion? Does
sound rather throaty! Do lions eat buffalo? Do wish I'd brought my
contacts. In that direction, Dear? Pass my camera, and stick . . . going
for a look.
(Bitch)

Back Dear . . . was I long? Don't think the animals were elephant, Dear.
The experience was exquisite. I could feel the noise of them: but each
time I got close, they'd run away. One pushed me over . . . lost my way;
lost my camera too. Gladys would've known what to do.
(. . .)

Heard you shouting Dear. Sorry I was so long. Oh dear, Dear. You've
spilled your drink! Seat's quite sticky.
(. . .)

Oh! And I remember . . . Gladys says she thinks they only have lion in this part of the park. You are quiet Dear.

(. . .)

Do lions and elephants get on well together Dear? Dear? Speak to me Dear.

(. . .)

(. . .)

(. . .)

Phil Manning

RUBY'S REASONS

Several years ago, we had returned home late one evening from our holidays. Everything appeared normal, before we went to bed, I took our dog Ruby for a walk along the lane, old habits die hard.

Ruby knew the route. When we approached old Mrs Simms' cottage, Ruby pulled me violently across the lane, this was odd but I thought little of it. Old Mrs Simms was leaning on her gate, enjoying the evening air. 'Evening Mrs Simms,' I called as was my manner, often stopping for a chat, but Ruby was in such a state, whimpering and growling. When I got back I told Jan about Ruby's odd behaviour and that I'd said hello to Mrs Simms as usual. We slept like two new-born babies back in our own bed.

Next morning we strolled with Ruby to the village stores, to restock vital provisions and to catch up on all the gossip. We commented on how good it was to be home, no place like it they say.

We chatted to Doris McKenzie, the shop's proprietor, she says, 'I don't suppose you'll know, poor old Mrs Simms passed on, poor old dear, she went peacefully in her sleep the day after you left. Lovely funeral we all attended, they did her proud. Her nephew Graham is moving into the cottage next week.'
We looked at each other in shock disbelief, we looked down at Ruby, she growled. Ruby obviously knew more than us.

P J Littlefield

SKIP TO THE LOO

We arrived in winter dark. The house was seriously old.

As in most family gatherings there was a wide age gap. To bridge the gap hospitality flowed.

The light switch was by the bedroom door, so I stumbled unlit to the door, every board creaked in a different key, the door adding a bass note.

Corridor mats rose in draughts. Something scuttled in the corner. A red eye winked, startling me. Idiot! Security light . . .

Two awkward steps, and as I teetered on the first, something cold wound round my neck with an icy follow-up. Who had left a window open. Damn that curtain damp from flapping in and out.

The top of the stairs gave a pistol shot as I reached it, so I stepped on hurriedly treading two boards which gave a donkey like Hee! Haw! Amazingly loud in the night.

Third door on the right, at last.

I put out my hand and started to grope for the light pull. My fingers seemed to have an echo. Scrape, scrape, scuffle, scuffle!

My heart didn't just stop, it leapt out and went back. My questing hand met an icy skeletal claw which seemed to pursue mine.

I pulled my arm back shuddering at the contact.

'Who's that?' quavered Great Aunt Sylvia, 'I've dropped my flipping torch.'

Di Bagshawe

PLUMBING THE DEPTHS

Tom Scott sat dejectedly at his laptop. His last novel had been a best-seller, the success that followed a powerful drug that he was still trying to kick start again and come up with the new book that he had promised his publishers. His brain had been barren of ideas for months. He sat there muttering to himself that he would give anything to come up with a good plot.

His head was throbbing from gazing vacantly at the blank screen, then without warning an advertisement flashed up before him:

Literary Plumbing Services
Writers Unblocked
Terms Arranged
E-mail: nick@hades.com

He sent an e-mail requesting the service and waited. At first the words started with a trickle as they slipped onto the screen. Then, manipulated by an unseen force, his fingers flew as the words gathered momentum and threw themselves from the keyboard to screen. Page after page of brilliant plot unfolded. The hours passed into days, days into weeks, as he sat hunched over the laptop. Delirious with excitement and lack of sleep, his eyes glittered feverishly. In his head he heard himself scream, as excruciating pain ripped through his overloaded brain. The last thing he saw before he blacked out were the closing words of the final chapter. His lifeless body slumped over the desk.

Now the narrative had gone from the screen and been replaced by what looked like a receipt:

Literary Plumbing Services
For Services Rendered
Account Paid In Full

Minutes later it slyly vanished.

Adrianne Jones

THE APPOINTMENT

It's happening again. Midnight, and the family have gone to bed. I'm still working, in the back room, my 'office' at home. The room is starting to darken, little by little; my sidelight is dimming; all the paraphernalia on my desk - computer, keyboard, telephone, papers, books - seem to be dissolving. Everything appears to be losing its comforting resistance, slowly, inexorably. The room is cooling down; I know this, but I don't feel the cold.

My doctor tells me I've been working too hard. I need a holiday. But I can't afford to ease off, not yet.

The hum of the computer has faded into a silence almost tangible. Now everything before me is vanishing, permeated with the dark. My world is becoming insubstantial. But somehow I'm still part of it; so I'm losing substance, too. I must be like a wraith. Yet I can still see, I can still sense; but there's nothing left to sense. There's just darkness, all around and within me. I am the burden of darkness, and it is I.

The air is dank and chill. I am standing, alone and naked. I can move, and my feet crunch on shingle. Sound. Water laps at my toes. There's movement in the dense darkness ahead, across the water. I can't see anything yet; but I can hear a measured, rhythmic 'plash . . . plash . . . plash'. Now every plash comes with a muffled creaking. In a moment I'll see.

Vivian John Beedle

The Enemy Within

No one knew why the barn door was always locked. The farmhouse itself was full of life. The family living there seemed without pretension. The history of the house was widely known with no sinister connotations. But the barn was never mentioned.

Little Jimmy and his playmates had once dared one another to peep through the cracks of the wooden door. They had all sensed the strange emptiness emanating from the darkness, shining out as they peered in. Shuddering, they scarpered across the field.

One night a traveller approached the farmhouse. The warm lights had attracted him. Windswept and tired from the driving rain he rested by the barn. Wiping the rain from his brow with his blue neck scarf he leaned for support on the barn door.

In the moment of hope in this traveller's heart for comfort and warmth at the warmly lit house the door of the barn gave way. His body was whirled into a pool of darkness. His mouth opened to cry out, but no sound came forth. He saw red eyes glowering at him in pain. In that moment of terror he knew that the effect of the cause he had left behind was waiting all the time for him here in the barn.

The next morning, as the light poured into the barn, a blue fragment of cotton - caught in the timber of the swinging door - fluttered hopelessly, as if trying to free itself from the horror of the night before.

Lorenza Cangiano

ALBERT RIP

Sitting with my husband, in this phoney 'respectful' silence of a cold funeral parlour, I shuddered. Surely we weren't the only hypocrites present. The reason we were here - *Albert*. Albert had been rather a loud boasting bear of a man. He regarded all men and women inferior, this attitude hadn't gained him too many friends. He also appeared to bully his little mouse of a wife, Olivia.

Trying to be neighbourly, we had invited the pair of them to supper, which Olivia declined, saying Albert did not approve of overeating or drinking too much. Similarly, Olivia was unable to attend a cosmetic demonstration. Albert disapproved of painted ladies!

In spite of all this, his sudden death had shocked us all. True to form he had left instructions, that he felt mankind would benefit greatly from his generous gift - his *brain*.

My reverie was abruptly interrupted by the arrival of a very, very, smartly dressed and groomed young lady. Wearing a very large, black straw hat, with dark glasses and eye veil. She carefully placed a little casket in front of us, before sitting, elegantly crossing her shapely legs and high heeled shoes. Every male present strained to get a better view.

After the short service, our mystery lady shook her head when offered the casket. I could swear that casket was shaking violently unaided.

Pushing aside her veil, our lady removed her glasses, smiled at us all and said, 'I don't think Albert approves of me!'
Olivia!

Ilean Greig

THE CELLAR

He'd hated being left alone with the cat, had in fact wanted it dead. So he'd poked it with Daddy's stick and when it had run under the couch, squealing and cowering, he'd attacked it again. This fresh assault had sent it running for the part open door; but to no avail, the boy's new-found power had made him braver than ever before. He'd slammed the door shut, trapping and killing the animal. Then it was quiet - too quiet, he'd been very scared and buried the limp black thing in the cellar under the stairs, in the darkness with his conscience.

No one ever suspected Ben all those years ago, they just assumed that Scratch had been run down by a car or just found a new owner prepared to pamper him even more than Daddy had, although that was hard to imagine. Scratch had been everything to Daddy, playmate and soulmate, whereas Ben had been an insult to his father's eyes, a millstone - and if it hadn't've been for the family allowance paying for Daddy's booze he would have been put in a home when Mum died.

Ben was only nine when Scratch disappeared. Since that day there had never been many living things of any sort in the vicinity of Ben's house. His fear of cats and his fear of death had both faded as his appetite for other lives had grown.

When Daddy disappeared on Ben's 16th birthday it would be an ordeal for Ben, all the questions over and over, but he wouldn't falter, all those years of torment, down there, in the cellar while Daddy lied upstairs. 'Yes, of course the boy's welfare is my main concern, that's why I let him stay at his aunt's house at Derrum-on-sea.' Ben had tried to call out once, to the lady from Social Services as she was leaving, but he hadn't heard Daddy come into the cellar. He was beaten badly that time and thrown into that place with Scratch. That was worse than the beating, he knew what was in there - still waiting for him, he'd torn at the door with his bare hands, although he knew this to be futile. Daddy had fitted a special latch that was self locking, so he had set to, kicking and screaming until Daddy could stand it no more - dragged him out, then beat him again until he was unconscious.

On Ben's 16th birthday he gave himself a special treat, he found a new use for Daddy's stick and then did himself a nice juicy leg of man for tea. Then it was time to finish the job in the cellar. The rest of Daddy was already in there with Scratch but his hole wasn't quite ready.

Ben was excited as he grabbed the spade he'd left resting against the door and descended the stairs to start digging again - he didn't hear the faint click of the special latch as the door swung to.

The last thing Ben heard, was his own wet rasping breath as the light went out.

Chris Collins-Reed

THE BRAMBLE

I sit here alone with all the house lights blazing and am afraid. The lengthening shadows of evening will soon turn to the all-engulfing darkness of night. The waving branches of trees bent to and fro by the breeze create a sinister picture beyond the windowpane.

The bramble whose cruel grip I had destroyed was like an enemy banished but vengeful.

It is well known the way in which the bramble catches hold and clings to a neglected spot. The keen gardener has to force a passage where they grow. The house was lovely, rambling and old and I had wanted to live there from the moment 'For Sale' appeared on the lawn.

All the garden needed was a fierce attack on bramble. The unsightly thing had gained a stranglehold and was blocking the greenhouse where my prize blooms would grow.

Not any more.

I had loaded the worthless bramble onto the rubbish tip and relaxed with a feeling of pride.

The bramble king had been banished from his stolen kingdom, the battle won.

Laughing and triumphant I ran to draw the heavy curtains against the night sky. Moonlight highlighted a bramble branch straggling the path.

All the lights shone through the open front door as rage propelled me forward to trip over another concealed bramble branch that gripped my ankle in a mean, cruel vice-like hold. I fell forward into darkness as my head hit a hard stone on the path.

Freda Grieve

MADDY

Leaving the big house, Maddy felt a rising panic as the high iron gates clanged behind her, she tried not to worry. All day, the men from the village had been gathering together; united in the task before them. As it became dusk they had made their way to the castle, armed with staves, knives and crucifixes holding aloft burning torches; intending to kill Dracula or burn him alive and stop the dreadful spate of killings.

The moon was high now casting eerie shadows through the trees, a twig snapped and for a second Maddy was transfixed with fear, then, she started to run for soon she would be home.

In the distance Maddy could see the torches and the castle was already burning; they must have caught Dracula and for a moment she felt safe.

Then, in the moonlight suddenly without warning, Dracula was barring her path, slowly he came towards her with arms outstretched and cape flying, he seemed to be floating on air.

Maddy could see the lights moving nearer towards her, men were shouting a warning but it was too late.

Maddy looked with horror on a face of incredible evil with eyes of red burning coals, the wide cruel lips turned into a vicious snarl; revealing long sharpened fangs. She tried to strike him with her umbrella but it slipped through her fingers clattering away on the wet cobblestones.

As Maddy stood paralysed with fright and as the cloak shrouded her in its darkness, she felt the sharp burning pain in her neck and then the sweet sickly smell of her own blood.

At last there came merciful oblivion.

Joan Hornett

SOFT MUSIC AND FIRELIGHT

Hidden by foliage, a figure stood watching the cottage on the far side of the field. It appeared deserted except for a thin wisp of smoke rising from the chimney. However the watching figure knew differently. The two-timing bitch was in there with Geoff.

As dusk turned to darkness, the figure skirted the field. Reaching the cottage and removing a key from a groove in the door frame, the figure carefully opened the door. The place was in darkness, the only sound, soft music coming from a room along the passage, and the unmistakable giggle of the two-timing bitch.

Quietly the figure moved towards the room. The door was ajar. The bitch was lying naked on a rug in front of the fire. Geoff was leaning over her running his tongue across her throat and down towards her breasts.

'I love it when you do that,' she giggled, pulling him down towards her. Suddenly Geoff slumped heavily onto her. Neither of them had heard or seen the figure raise the knife and plunge it into Geoff's back.

'Geoff! Get off! You're hurting me,' cried the bitch. She struggled to push him from her. Then she felt something warm and sticky trickling off his back onto her arm. She gave an extra push and he started to slip off her body. She saw the knife glittering in the firelight as it descended towards her exposed body. She tried to scream, but the sound got no further than her throat.

Sue Davan

AT NIGHT TIME

Lady Challendar had died suddenly and her husband - Lord Robert was devastated and inconsolable. Her body was laid to rest in the family vault, in all her finery, a beautiful dress, a tiara and other jewellery. This was reported in the local newspapers and caught the eye of local villain - Bill Grundy, who decided to steal it.

That night Grundy crept through the grounds until he reached the vault. He entered the tomb and barely saw the rows of stone coffins. Soon he found the newest one and with a struggle managed to slide the heavy lid aside.

He gasped as he saw her ladyship laying there. She looked to be asleep. Losing no time Grundy grabbed the tiara then tore off the necklace and earrings and reached for the sparkling ring. He cursed as he tried unsuccessfully to remove it.

Giving up he withdrew from his pocket a knife, he placed her finger on the side of the coffin and cut the outer skin, blood immediately welled to the surface. His sawing action caused more blood to gush out. Then with a deathly scream Grundy recoiled as the figure started to rise. Yelling, Grundy dropped his ill-gotten gains and fled into the night. The sequel was Lady Challendar recovered from her comatose state and lived a long and happy life.

Lord Robert was delighted to have his wife restored to him and advertised a reward for the person/persons responsible, but no one came forward to claim.

Terry Daley

THE WOOD

Terror gripped hold of her with icy fingers as she walked along the path. The menacing wood was full of whispers and unseen eyes that seemed to penetrate her very soul.

Her stomach churned and her hair stood on end, like soldiers standing to attention. Her heart beating so hard and fast she thought it would burst through her chest.

The deafening silence was almost overwhelming.

Slowly, she put one foot in front of the other, eyes wide, ears alert.

How she yearned to be cosy and safe at home, sitting beside a warm, welcoming fire. The darkness outside unable to permeate through into her sanctuary. The light within holding it back with an unseen power.

Crack! A twig snapped.

Someone, or something, was lurking in the depths of the shadows.

Like a frightened rabbit she froze, paralysed by fear.

Overpowered by panic, she began to run. Branches scratched her arms and face and tugged and tore her clothes, but she dared not stop. Intense terror mounted as she heard the unseen, unknown being right behind her.

Despair spurred her on. Not far now.

Suddenly, she broke free from the clutches of the wood. In the distance a welcome light - her one hope.

But, to her utmost horror, her one salvation was extinguished before her eyes, like a candle being blown out, plunging her into the depths of blackness that enveloped her in a shroud of darkness - forever.

Vanessa Bell

FOOD FOR THOUGHT

The freezing fog crept like leprosy up the cliff to its final resting place; the graveyard. A fitting place for what was to occur.

He moved position. He was hungry and cold even through his winter coat. He shuddered as freezing droplets fell from his coat to the ground. Wishing his visitors would arrive so he could get his job done he took out his weapons and sharpened them a little more, his cut must be quick and clean. He wanted no blood on his new coat.

A smell of death and putrefied flesh filled the air as the inhabitants slept on unaware of what was to come!

He thought of moving on as impatience overpowered him. Maybe his visitors weren't coming after all. Suddenly a light appeared in the church, he peered through a window. Two men were talking. Time to make his move! Without breathing or being seen he entered. As quick as a flash he sliced into the throats of both victims. Its job was done. Now he must move quickly and quietly as he heard voices again. Maybe it was the choir? Hastily he picked up more cadavers and ventured into the macabre night.

His wife and children were pleased to see him as they too were very hungry. It didn't matter to them that their father was a murderer, he was only providing food for the table. He had done well tonight bringing home six juicy mice as the owlets took some feeding!

D Threlfall

E-MAIL FROM HELL

Conrad wrote of a heart of darkness. The horror, the horror. What was relevant then, is it so in this day and age? Stoker stirred the deep, dark fears of the unknown, but the vampire has changed, the setting has changed, no more the gothic underworld, the jungle also retreats.

Today the terror lurks in the urban setting, the monsters have become the corporate giants, what price humanity as these faceless empires strive ever onward, towards their goal of financial domination.

No more lurking in murky, dank cellars, hiding from the sunlight, resting in a coffin, waiting for sunset. Nowadays the vampires wear Armarni suits, they meet up in boardrooms, make plans to suck the life-force in fine style, from multitudes at once.

From there on in, the word goes down, down the line, out and onwards spreading like a malignant virus. You sit at your desk, a message pops up, 'You got mail'. What causes the cold sweat to start trickling oh so slowly down your spine?

You've had hundreds of E-mails, day after day, why worry? Is it because of the rumours doing the rounds? Is it because this memo has come from somewhere you've never had one from before? The anger at your fear only increases the sweat and palpitations.

The egg timer on the screen seems to take forever to open the E-mail. Finally, there it is, your worst nightmare confirmed. Yeah, it's drafted in 'corporate speak' but it still means the same thing. A business proposal, an amalgamation, a view to a positive future. Yeah, not yours though. You're finished.

Movies, books, zines and comics. For years I've followed and loved the horror genre. Yet nothing has ever chilled my spine like that one single word. Nearly 50 years old, had one heart attack already, got heart disease, now . . . redundancy!

John Carter

CRUCIFIXION

The sun was setting as the others left the church. Janice was pleased as she could now spend time tidying up her Easter display of daffodils and tulips. The old bulbs in the roof gave off just enough light as she arranged the happy faces.

Though glad to be free of her companions' chatter, the silence hung in the air; not peaceful, almost sinister. Clearing dead foliage from the carpet, she shivered and determined to finish as quickly as possible and return to her cottage fireside, with a pot of tea and blanket over her tired knees.

Then, just out of vision, something white rushed past her and she noticed, to her horror, that a key had appeared in the lock of the little blue door leading up to the bells. It began to turn, noiselessly and the door opened slowly.

'Who's there?' she stammered, but there was no reply.

Suddenly, the main door slammed behind her.

'Help me!' Janice shouted, but got her arm caught in one of the bell ropes.

It too started to move - up and down - but there was no sound from the giant bell above. The hollow eyes of the Gargoyles, below the ceiling, were alive, burning brightly; their angry faces glaring at her.

Janice heard a dripping noise behind her and swung round quickly. She covered her mouth to stifle the scream inside her.

The flowers had rearranged themselves into a red cross and, below the pedestal, was a pool of dark sticky blood.

Mark Rasdall

THE KISS

It was the coldest of all winters that year. The heavily laden snow had drifted across the epitaphs of the village cemetery bestowing each of their occupants a secondary burial.

The icy air and silence also drifted into the church enveloping the two within, the bereaved and newly deceased.

Vigilant candles flickered their spectral existence upon the corpse, towering on tall pedestals like medieval guardians. Even in mortality his beloved was beautiful. He approached closer, his footsteps echoed on the vaults below as if all the spirits had chosen to follow him. He felt their breath about him but it was just the chill of the wind.

He stood beside the ebony casket transfixed by her ashen face, he remembered kissing those once warm lips that were now tainted with the bluish hue of death. Yet in a macabre sense he found those lips voluptuous.

A wreath of ghost-white lilies shrouded her motionless breast, their fading blooms entwining her almost transparent fingers. Tonight would be their last alone for soon she would join the others outside. Wiping away a few of his tears he lent over knowing he had to have one final kiss. His tears fell effortlessly upon her, her lips made moist by their touch but while pulling away he found that he couldn't. He tried again, till the skin from his own lips oozed with blood but he was frozen to her and there he was found in the morning, embraced in a kiss and also dead.

Maria Colvin

THE NIGHTMARE

It was a nightmare. He had been having the same one since he was six years old and had become separated from his parents on a skiing holiday. It had been cold on the mountain. With just the whistle of the wind for company. They had found him quickly, but occasionally the dream came back to remind him of that awful day.

This time however, it was different. This time although he was lost in the snow and through the trees he could see people and dogs searching further down the mountain. Strange that they should be looking for him there, while at the top he was searching for something himself, but he wasn't sure what.

He felt strange, the thinness of the air he supposed. He was cold. He needed to wake up. And he would if he could just find what it was he was searching for. The alarm would ring and it would be time to get up and do what he did best. Time to get up and fly the large fighter planes that he had wanted to fly from the age of ten.

He spun round in the snow, eyes darting everywhere. He spied a shape in the snow, dashed over and scrapped the snow away. He caught his breath, it was part of a plane. His plane. Frantically he scrapped more snow away and found himself staring down at a body - his body. He realised at last that his nightmare had come true.

Pat Rissen

WAS IT HIM?

That night was one I will always remember, when from sleeping peacefully, I suddenly felt the hairs on the back of my neck spring into life, and my whole body felt wooden and lifeless. I could not move any part of myself, except my eyes, which darted frantically in my urge to move an arm or a leg!

Of course, I had heard the expression 'paralysed with fear', and now I knew what it was like, as I lay in bed, facing the window, trying desperately to move a limb, with a sense of foreboding that someone, or something, was stood behind me, by the bedroom door, watching.

There was no sound, just a perception of being observed as my breathing began to get laboured, and panic was setting in. The darkness felt like it was closing in on me, as still I could not move. I wanted to cry out, but no words came from within, only my eyes seemed alive, and much as I wanted to be able to turn over, my lifeless body would not let me.

Could this be my departed husband, who was paying one last visit? The only way he could now, to watch and care from the other side, after the suddenness of his death, to make sure all was well with his family. Once that thought entered my head, I felt life begin to stir in my numbed limbs, and I could turn to face the door to see.

No one.

Pamela Sears

THE LOTTERY BUG

Sam sat down exhausted at the foot of the cellar steps and lit a cigarette, his fifteenth of the day. He kept a tally to make one packet last all day, leaving him enough to accompany a six-pack of beer for the evening game on TV.

The hot, sticky afternoon was spent spraying a tank of insecticide over hundreds of cockroaches that now littered the damp cellar floor. The pleasure of watching them squirm in a DDT bath and the sound of their carapace shells crunching beneath his boots was his idea of a sick bonus to a lousy job.

A radio playing in the kitchen at the head of the stairs suddenly announced the winning numbers in the Florida state lottery. Sam took a line every week and pulled a ticket from the top pocket of his 'Bugs-R-Gon' overalls.

He gazed at his numbers, ticking them off mentally one by one, and found they were all correct!

'All correct,' he screamed excitedly, 'I've done it. I'm a multi-bloody-millionaire. No more lousy, rotten bugs, no more . . .'

The ticket was suddenly snatched from his sweaty fingers. 'That will do very nicely,' said a deep, raspy voice.

Sam turned with gaping jaw to see the towering figure of a gargantuan, black cockroach. It separated his bewildered head from his shoulders as if it were dead-heading a rose with secateurs.

'Compensation,' it said smugly.

Martin Richmond

THE MODEL-MAKER

He has been working for years, eyesight getting worse as he stares closely at his work. His withered hands still have the control of a master craftsman, painting every detail so fine with a horsehair brush. He does not have time to stop and admire his work, moving quickly onto the next subject before the paint has time to dry.

If you were to look closely yourself, you would be amazed. Politicians, royalty, celebrities - each has a miniature likeness. He stores them in a giant display case, every day subtly altering their position. It is only by looking down from above that you can make out what these tiny figures are standing on - a map of the world.

Above the hushed sounds of the workshop, you can hear thousands of voices, like the original Tower of Babel. Each is coming from a TV or radio tuned to a different station, feeding into his room the thousands of events that make up daily life.

Now he has opened the cabinet, gently picking up the tiny figure of a leading politician. In the real world, this man is about to make an important speech that could shape the world. The model-maker's hand slips, sending the point of the knife into the model's chest.

'And finally, the main story tonight. Michael Jones, who many regarded as a future leader of this country, has collapsed and died of a heart attack during a press conference this afternoon.'

Andrew Fisher

CAVES

Hearing footsteps behind her, the small girl turned quickly, no one was there, unless they were hiding in the dark shadows of the caves. Strange noises filtered through the corridors, unnerving her even more. Who or what could be following her every step?

Echoes of smugglers on a daring mission to import silk and rum whispered gratingly into her ears. She began to feel like she had been left alone in the world and the shadow-shapes were out to get her. Maybe they hid one-eyed pirates or waiting wolves, hungry for the blood of a small innocent child.

Her fear was compounded by the occasional flashing of lights in the distance and shuffling movements of what she perceived as groups of zombies, herding together, waiting to trap their next victim and turn them into walking carcasses too. She was getting very scared now.

Millicent began to walk quickly, her heartbeat so fast she envisaged apocalyptic horses galloping across open plains, steam blasting from their demonic mouths and flames coming from their hooves.

Catching up with the suspected zombies she noticed the light of day behind them. Given the chance to see clearly where she was going she ran past them, into clear space and onto green grass. Catching her breath she said, 'Dad, can we come back to St Clement's caves again one day?'

'Of course,' her dad said, 'Hastings isn't too far away.

Danny Coleman

THE CONDEMNED

It was a shorter walk than I anticipated. That is from my dark, dingy little cell to the scaffold where the noose was waiting. Two warders on each side were leading me towards where the rope was dangling aimlessly, next to a priest who was reading something or other out aloud; I was too scared to know what it was, or even care. He was probably reading the Last Rites for my benefit, but I wasn't sure.

As the priest mumbled on, somebody placed the hood over my head, and everything went pitch-black. I could still hear the priest, but nothing else, as the hood was beginning to make it difficult for me to breathe properly, a problem that shouldn't last long.

Suddenly something touched the top of my head, and slid tightly down over my face to my neck and tightened so much, that now I had difficulty breathing at all. I was so scared. The footsteps of the two warders now receded into the background, they had done their work for me now. The noose was pulled even tighter than it was before. Then, the priest had stopped whatever it was he was reading out and there was just silence.

God help my soul! Oh no, the wooden trapdoor beneath my feet has gone and . . .!

Christopher Higgins

AMANDA'S WATER-COLOUR

Amanda settled down in the grass and picked up her paintbrush. This would be her best effort yet, she wanted it to be perfect. She gazed at the picturesque hills in the distance and began to paint.

The picture quickly took shape, but Amanda wished that it had more depth, there was something missing somehow . . .

After a while she stopped and stretched, the hours of painting were beginning to play tricks on her eyes, it seemed to her that the hills looked oddly flat and were an unnatural shade of green, even the sky seemed strange and washed out. Amanda jumped up as she felt a wave of fear in her stomach - the scenery before her was slowly changing, becoming hazy and dream-like, colours turning translucent and watery. In disbelief she looked down at her painting and was shocked to see that the picture wasn't what she had painted at all, in fact, it looked real, like a photograph. She shakily reached out to touch it and with dawning horror, realised that her hand had become two-dimensional and unreal looking and she could only watch helplessly as she herself started to become as blurry and featureless as the surrounding scenery . . .

They never found any trace of Amanda except for a strange water-colour painting. It was a scene of the nearby hillside, painted in flowing pastel colours, and hidden in the picture was an image of the artist herself with her mouth wide open, frozen in a silent scream!

Ashley Cairns

THE ALABASTER HAND

Linda looked round the tidy flat. She was going shopping. She walked through the market. Suddenly she saw something attractive. It was a smooth alabaster hand, the fingers stretched out for rings. It would look good on her new dressing table. She went home and arranged it on a stand.

That night, Lisa went to bed with her book. When she turned the light out she thought she saw the hand move. There was a strange light over it. She thought it must be the moon. There was no moon! The hand rose up and floated towards her. She was very frightened. She closed her eyes. The hand stroked her hair. Lisa opened her eyes to see the hand floating back on its stand. She jumped out of bed, and ran to the dressing room. Locking the door, she crept into bed, and waited. There was a gentle tapping on the door. A tinkling laugh and the handle moved. Then silence.

The next day Lisa washed and dressed, then opened the door. The hand was quite still on its stand. Lisa lit a fire, tried to take the rings off. They were suddenly tight. She took the hand which felt soft and threw it on the fire. There was a terrible scream, then all was quiet. it was gone. Lisa breathed a sigh of relief.

Betty Puddefoot

AN EDUCATION IN CANNIBALISM

John sat outside the headmaster's office, sweating and cold.

He remembered the words of the headmaster. 'If you stand before me again, I'll eat you up!'

An image of this formed in John's mind. The headmaster, snatching John's hand, feeding it into his old mouth, those sharp teeth working their way up to John's wrist, then elbow, then shoulder, then neck, then face, John, not moving, trying to scream but nothing coming out, only able to *watch*, the climbing horror . . .

The anger felt during his fight with Paul was tamed by the dread he now experienced. Even his fear at being caught was overcome by his present terror. The more he *struggled* against this fear, the more he *became* afraid.

He could feel an actual sensation of fear in his body, a fluttering in his stomach, a sense of restlessness. It reminded him of when his grandad died, him grieving, his brother telling him what the worms would do.

'I'll be good,' John screamed at the teacher. 'Please, not the headmaster.'

He should never have looked up about 'Cannibalism'. He should never have watched those videos with his brother. That was when he broke; to be *here* without having *seen,* he could have taken that.

Why was it that boys who were called twice to the headmaster's office were never seen again?

John froze as he heard the voice of the headmaster call out to Mrs Black. 'Send John in quickly. It's almost lunchtime.'

John's bladder gave way.

Allen Baird

THE LONG WAY HOME

Aimee was driving home from work and out of the corner of her eye she saw an old lady with bags of shopping. Aimee shouted 'Would you like a lift?'

'Yes please,' said the old lady as she got into the car.

'Where shall I drop you?' Aimee asked hoping it was not too far away.

'Next left, about a mile down the road please.'

Aimee groaned inwardly it would take her forever to get back on the dual carriageway.

She drove about a mile and a half when the old lady put her hand up to stop the car.

'There are no houses around here,' Aimee said.

'I only live around the corner,' she replied.

Aimee closed the car door, looked up but the old lady had disappeared.

She drove all around but there were no houses anywhere.

'That was very weird,' she thought. 'I've driven up and down but I can't see her.'

She was deep in thought as she drove back to the junction, when a policeman stopped the car.

'You can't go home this way, there has been a terrible accident if you had been five minutes earlier, it could have been you.'
.

'It would have been if I had not given an old lady a lift up the road.'

'Nobody has lived up there since old Mrs Davies was knocked down on this road years ago,' the policeman said.

Aimee felt sick, was the old lady she had given a lift to, a ghost or her guardian angel?

D A Fieldhouse

THE WINDOW

The mist crept in, grey and damp, as he trudged along the narrow road.
He walked slowly on the rough surface, his mind on many things.
No traffic had passed this way for a very long time. He, himself, had not
been here for many years but now he felt compelled to return.

Something lured him to see again the old cottage at the head of the
valley. It was a ruin now, windows broken, all except one. This window
that drew him like a magnet to come back. He shivered as the mist
closed in around him and he quickened his step.

Suddenly, there it was, the cottage looming out of the gloom, a broken
gate hanging on one hinge swinging idly. Undergrowth growing all
around the old walls and windows gaunt without glass. All broken
except one.

His eyes were drawn to it and he remembered that day long ago, now a
distant memory. He remembered the face at that window and a cold
chill ran through him as he drew closer.

Could he look? Had he walked all this way for nothing. The window
was dirty, the years had taken their toll. He took several steps closer and
then suddenly there it was! A sad face stared out, motionless, a face
from the past.

It looked past him to the distant hills beyond.

The lonely hills, partly covered now with a thick mist, he stood for a
few moments before he turned and slowly walked away.

The window and the cottage receded in the gathering darkness.

A H Thomson

THE VISITOR

Most of us have experienced the heightening of the senses that comes when darkness falls. Having worked on shift for over thirty years, I am more than familiar with this.

A building of 150 years of age was designated as the smoking area as it was away from the plants.

One night, one of the technicians (Jim) went over to find his mate Matty who was at the bottom of the stairs shaking. Matty was a great big bear of a man who nobody messed with.

'See if he's still up there, Jim,' asked Matty.
'Who?' queried Jim.
'That there fella in the green overalls!' Matty replied.
'Settle down mate! Which fella?'

Jim climbed the stairway and both were extremely nervous. On entering the smoke room they found it empty. Matty then told Jim that after finishing his supper he went over for a crafty drag. Inside the room was a large figure with his back to him which was dressed in green overalls which had a hood on it like a ski suit.

Matty lit up and tried to engage the visitor in small talk. Having had no answer Matty settled down to enjoy his cigarette then the figure turned round - it had no face! Matt was scared rigid although he was a tough cookie and not easily shaken.

A year later Matty was killed on site by an accidental slip from a roof, where his face was also badly disfigured.

Who was the visitor? Had he brought Matt a message of the future?

S Murphy

NEVER BY MOONLIGHT

Dark clouds threatened to engulf the waning moon as Ewan Moray strode over dead heather on a forlorn moor, bound for Falconrigg Stone Circle. The regulars at his holiday inn had spoken of the Circle as an ominous place, seldom visited by daylight and never by moonlight. They added that if you counted the stones you would never have the same answer twice. Ewan had resolved scornfully to defy superstition.

After a trek that seemed longer than the distance indicated on the signpost, he saw two great upright stones like gateposts. He entered hesitantly and stood among the blue moon-shadows cast by the slightly smaller stones that ringed him. He was aware of a sudden icy chill: aware, too, of an uncanny sense of being watched malevolently.

Feverishly he counted the stones. Twenty-four. Again. Twenty-six! Again? He must. Twenty-five! Panic seized him, and he fled. He did not flee far. A few minutes brought him back to those great gateway stones. Once again, he felt compelled to count the stones, over and over, over and over . . .

At the inn they awaited his return. They waited in vain.

E Margaret Kidd

Auld Reekie

My name is Professor Benoit Mandelbröt and I am a research metaphysical psychologist: a 'ghostbuster'. I am speaking to you from the dungeons of Edinburgh Castle, where myself and my colleagues, Doctors Escher and Möbius are engaged in a search for Scotland's spirit world.

In our quest to penetrate the veil we have employed the latest scientific measuring devices - poltergeist CCTV, phantom radio carbon dating, internet seances and ectoplasmic laser spectroscopy.

Unfortunately, the instruments are malfunctioning. Perhaps the Castle's granite walls are inhibiting signals. I will try to recalibrate them, if . . . you . . . just . . . bear . . . with . . . me.

I must confess to being perturbed by this turn of events. I have lost contact with my two colleagues who are located on the Castle battlements. The lights on my equipment are short-circuiting, I'm losing power . . . the temperature is dropping rapidly, the cold is seeping into my bones.

Can't see, stumbling about blindly, wildly grasping for something solid. The walls closing in, oozing plasma, blood, fear.

Where are those moans coming from? Who are you? Where are you? Eh? What? Why do you want me? What do you want of me? Groans, sighs. Stop it! You're hurting me. Not my throat, pains in my side, cold in my stomach's pit . . . eh? Hello . . . hello . . . losing contact with the outside world . . . with the upper world . . .

John Doyle

AND THEN THERE WAS MAN

It was New Year's Day, year two thousand.

So little did the world know that the Devil had come back to Earth. The Angel Michael had sent his henchmen to overcome the people. They turned out the light of the sun and dark storm clouds covered every inch of the Earth. Flames shot from potholes in the street. The ground shook as earthquakes rattled every city. People were running around in panic. Streaks of lightning lit up the now dark sky - the air was cold as ice. Even the strongest believers had tears in their eyes.

In Rome the Pope held a prayer service in the main square of St Peter's. On the beach of Tahiti, angels and demon armies faced each other in the final battle. Flames of fire shot back and forth as each fired their only weapon.

Here it was, the start of Satan's first Millennium.

The next thousand years God would take the back seat and the Devil sit on the gold throne.

Colin Allsop

BONFIRE NIGHT

He'd been planning it for months and looking forward to bonfire night. The children would enjoy it. Children love a bonfire . . . they might even forget that their grandfather had no fireworks if he could make it big enough. Since he'd lost his job, money was too short to be wasted on fireworks . . . it was burning money . . . but a bonfire . . . that was free. Fireworks are dangerous anyway . . . and bonfires, come to that. He'd have to make sure the children stayed well clear . . . he didn't want anything happening to the children.

'Stealing company property,' Bates had said it was. Instant dismissal. Just a few offcuts to make little Jenny a doll's house for Xmas. They would have been burnt anyway. You'd think after twenty years they'd let a chap have a few bits of scrap timber, wouldn't you? It gave old Bates the chance to save a few quid in redundancy payments. Still, he was better out of it. Since Bates took over last year, the firm had been going downhill. It was doomed now.

He could see Bates sitting up there in his office . . . fiddling the figures . . . lining his pockets . . . Guy Fawkes on top of his pile.

Hedgehogs . . . that's the trouble . . . they hibernate inside woodpiles. He wouldn't want to cook an innocent hedgehog. But Bates? That was different. He was not so innocent.

The match flared and with a whoosh, the flame gobbled up the trail of petrol that ran into the timber yard.

'Hi, kids. Come and look at this bonfire!'

David Kellard

THE DARK CABIN

After the accident, they had given him morphine and the pain had lessened until he was dozing off, comfortably drowsy in a quiet harbour.

Vaguely, he remembered being stretchered ashore to a local hospital for treatment. There wasn't much memory of the treatment but now the pain had gone and he felt in top condition and guessed he'd been shipped back to the boat. Nothing much to worry about, after all. He began to dream.

This cabin seemed abysmally dark, his berth rather cramped and airless. Perhaps it was the lack of air which had aroused him, ending his dream.

He fumbled for a box of matches in his jacket pocket, struck one, and immediately sucked in a lungful of acrid fumes. Knowing at once that his dream still persisted because the coffin he had been dreaming about still enclosed him but now the lid was screwed down tight.

The sudden thought crossed his mind that he was buried alive. Gasping for breath, he knew he had to wake up. He had to get rid of this terrible dream.

The effects of morphine were moderating, the pain returning and, in the darkness, there was something slimy crawling over his face.

William Sheffield

HIDDEN AGENDAS

They all knew what she didn't know. How could they be so cold and calculating? It all boiled down to money, or did it? Perhaps more to it than that, espionage and hidden truths. No one listened to her regarding the concerns she had been brought into by a so-called friend of her late Aunt, not even the police. How was it the doctor did not know, he hadn't seen her fourteen days prior to her death? Also old age on death certificate left question marks! What sort of people were these friends of her late Aunt. As she had never been to visit her late Aunt, nor got to see her, it was one long nightmare, which had lasted five years. Now, as she read the contents of a letter from her late Aunt's Solicitor, pertaining to have been written by her late Aunt, it was all too much for her, she was gutted. A troublemaker, she was not, someone had done a good job with hidden agendas and she had been condemned from the grave.

Josephine Paris

A Vegetarian's Nightmare

I knew that dropping in for a full English breakfast was a mistake.

The ketchup resembled tidal mud that trapped my wellies. I looked around anxiously for higher ground, in front of me was the bacon formed like a giant switchback, no possibilities there but just behind me, to my left, I spotted the French fries, piled on each other like the strata of a cliff. The structure was fatty but supportive. I managed somehow to get some hand grips and gained the summit, exhausted. Surveying the landscape, the prospects weren't good. I thought I might be able to reach the edge of the plate via the sausages, circumventing the eggs that gleamed like spaceships in the centre of glistening glaciers curling over the bacon.

Summing up courage, I decided at some risk to confront the tomatoes in order to avoid the eggs. Unfortunately in descending, my foot slipped and I landed heavily in an overwhelming slosh of tomato. Forcing myself to keep calm and somewhat bruised, I slithered around until my head was above the mess. I gasped for air. Thank goodness the sausages were right beside me! Over-eager to gain my freedom, I began to stumble over them, caught my foot between two of the sausages, lost my hold and found myself hanging upside down . . .

I came to, to find myself disorientated and with a blinding headache - but I was safe!

A full English breakfast - never again!

Deirdré Hill

GRAVE VISIT

In a small country churchyard one sunny afternoon, I was searching for a name on a gravestone, looking up my family tree. I gradually made my way to the end of the pathway, leading to some steps that were through a small gate. As I went to walk away I felt a shiver run down my spine, as if I was being watched. I turned to look and saw a child about ten years old, she was wearing a sailor dress and a white ribbon in her hair, and dark stockings and shoes. She was telling me to go away. I felt quite shaken by this. She kept waving to me to go away, it was a very spooky feeling. I made my way back to my husband.
He said, 'Whatever is the matter?'
I said, 'We must go now, please.'

All the way home I felt as though she was watching me. It made me very uneasy. My husband was starting to worry. I felt quite numb.

Well, the next evening, I was reading our local paper, when to my surprise on the front page was the heading 'Country church burnt down.' Same church, same day! I was being asked to leave the churchyard by that little spirit girl. Who was she? Did she save my life?

Julie Dawe

GRAVE NEWS

'Help,' came the feeble cry, reverberating through the cold damp fog, Maggie's blood froze in her veins, her feet refused to move.

The wall to her left bordered the churchyard. A place she hated passing even on a sunny day, let alone a night-time pea-souper like this. This cry for help was just too much, it unnerved her.

'Help,' the cry came again. She was sure it was coming from inside the churchyard. She couldn't go in, she just couldn't. Yet, if someone really was in trouble and she didn't help she would never forgive herself.

Slowly, her leaden feet moved towards the gate, opened it and started up the path. The cry came again, not far away, to her left.

The beam of her torch before her, she crept inch by inch towards the sound. The beam fell on a newly-dug grave. Empty, yet the cry came again, seemingly from the hole itself. This was too much for Maggie. Screaming, she turned tail and ran and didn't stop until she had reached the safety of her own home.

The next morning she dragged her mother along to look at the grave. There was no open grave.
'Hysteria' her mother said.

On reaching home the phone rang. Her mother started crying saying, 'Your gran died at 8 o'clock last night.'
Just about the time Maggie had passed the churchyard.
'Where will she be buried, Mum?' she asked.
'Why, in our churchyard of course, where her family are.' she said.

Dora Watkins

DINNER FOR TWO

Surprisingly, when I came home from school after a long day of total boredom, the house was quiet, usually I can hear Mum and Dad rowing from the corner of the street, which in turn starts next door's dog off! Dad is an undertaker - quite good, so they say.

Mum, well, she's just Mum.

Today though, there was a peacefulness about the house that I had not felt in twelve years, well, nearly thirteen, it's my birthday next week.

I could smell dinner cooking as I dumped my bag in the hall, Dad shouted to find out what sort of day I'd had.

'Usual,' I replied, 'where's Mum?'

'Oh, she'll be joining us for dinner,' he yelled from the depths of the kitchen.

I continued up the stairs thinking about what excuse I could use that coming weekend to get to the party at Nicky's - everyone was going.

'Dinner's up!'

I bounded down the stairs to a table set for two. 'Where's Mum?' I asked to Dad's back as he went back into the kitchen.

'She'll be here soon,' he said as he brought the plates in.

I tucked in, it looked so good, and smelt delicious.

'New recipe, Dad?' I said admiringly, 'what is it?'

'Heart, liver and kidneys,' he replied, 'so nice of your mother to join us and be so quiet for a change. The rest's in the freezer for tomorrow.'

I rushed from the table to the freezer, and sure enough, there was Mum, smiling contentedly with a gash down her middle. Ice clinging to her skin.

Chrissi

CODE WORD

They had him in their power. The clever Englishman who could interpret British codes into German.

Graham Hollis had landed overnight thinking he was to meet a fellow British Officer. It was when he saw the grim Gestapo giant moving towards him in the murky airfield he realised how he had been deceived.

It was too late now - or was it? The Nazi agent's thick glasses were suddenly enlarged, lit by a weird sulphurous gleam that acted like a searchlight. *'Aaach!'* screamed the fat German in a tone that was even more peculiar. Then 'Grandma!' exclaimed Hollis seeing all at once a vision of his grandmother neé Battenberg of Dresden who'd been married to Kurt - a decent enough bloke.

'Don't worry, Laddie, he'll die' she chuckled. Just translate 'ghost' into German. We're expecting him. He always hated poor Kurt.'

Great dollops of rain made the airfield a canopy of silver arrows. Then it stopped. The Gestapo agent leered and Grannie had gone back to eternity and hopefully to Grandpa Kurt. Herr Schmidt's glasses contracted and then bulged with a menacing ferocity. He lurched forward towards Hollis.

'Who vere you talking to just now?' he demanded in his thick accent. Vot vos that code? Tell me!'
'G H for ghost!' spat Graham Hollis on a near-hysterical note -
'Gespenst!' and it was then the bolt of lightning struck Herr Schmidt, killing him.

'Hallelujah!' shrilled Hollis as he boarded a Spitfire for home, thirsting for revenge.

Ruth Daviat

Rocking Chair *And* The Rosary

'Is there something troubling you?'

'Well yes, you know you asked me to make a start on the house clearance at Mum's old place? Well I decided to stay over last night while you were away, and in the late evening, I was sat quietly in the living room with the door closed and the fire on low. There was a chill in the room so I stood up and walked towards the gas fire to turn it up slightly.

Standing alongside the fireplace was Mum's old rocking chair; out of the corner of my eye I swear I saw it move, just as if someone was steadying it to sit down. I stepped back in half-surprise not knowing what to think, and as I stood and watched in silence, the cushions in the chair took shape as if someone was sitting there.

I stood there in total silence and disbelief, the chair started a slow, gentle rocking motion just like Mum was sitting there. I heard a half-mumbled voice in prayer just like Mum used to do. It's as if she is still there, living out her old routine.

I closed my eyes in disbelief and said a silent prayer,
'Mother if this is really you, please give me a sign to let me know you are really there.' I stood there quiet and still, and when I opened my eyes the rocking chair was motionless and still and on the cushions was Mother's old rosary.

Robert Waggitt